The Tunnel

Ernesto Sábato was born on 24 June 1911 in Rojas, Argentina. He obtained his PhD in Physics from the Universidad Nacional de La Plata, but in 1945 he abandoned his career in science to dedicate himself exclusively to writing and painting. In 1948, after being rejected by several editors in Buenos Aires, Sábato published *El Túnel* in France's *Sur* magazine, where it was read by Albert Camus, who commissioned the novel for Gallimard. Thomas Mann and Graham Greene quickly announced their admiration for the novel. It has been further translated into more than ten languages and has become an international bestseller. Sábato's other novels include *On Heroes and Tombs* (1961) and *The Angel of Darkness* (1974).

Colm Tóibín was born in Ireland in 1955. He is the author of six novels, including *The Blackwater Lightship* and *The Master*, both of which were shortlisted for the Booker Prize and *Brooklyn*, which won the Costa Novel Award. He is also the author of two short story collections, *Mothers and Sons* and *The Empty Family*.

ERNESTO SÁBATO

The Tunnel

*Translated from the Spanish by Margaret Sayers Peden
with an Introduction by Colm Tóibín*

PENGUIN BOOKS

PENGUIN CLASSICS

Published by the Penguin Group
Penguin Books Ltd, 80 Strand, London WC2R 0RL, England
Penguin Group (USA) Inc., 375 Hudson Street, New York, New York 10014, USA
Penguin Group (Canada), 90 Eglinton Avenue East, Suite 700, Toronto, Ontario, Canada M4P 2Y3
(a division of Pearson Penguin Canada Inc.)
Penguin Ireland, 25 St Stephen's Green, Dublin 2, Ireland (a division of Penguin Books Ltd)
Penguin Group (Australia), 250 Camberwell Road, Camberwell, Victoria 3124, Australia
(a division of Pearson Australia Group Pty Ltd)
Penguin Books India Pvt Ltd, 11 Community Centre, Panchsheel Park, New Delhi – 110 017, India
Penguin Group (NZ), 67 Apollo Drive, Rosedale, Auckland 0632, New Zealand
(a division of Pearson New Zealand Ltd)
Penguin Books (South Africa) (Pty) Ltd, 24 Sturdee Avenue, Rosebank, Johannesburg 2196, South Africa

Penguin Books Ltd, Registered Offices: 80 Strand, London WC2R 0RL, England

www.penguin.com

First published in Spanish as *El Tunel* by Sur, Buenos Aires 1948
First published in Great Britain by Jonathan Cape 1988
First published in Penguin Classics 2011

2

Copyright © Ernesto Sábato 1948, 1982
English translation copyright © Random House, Inc., 1988
Introduction copyright © Colm Tóibín, 2011

Set in 11.45/14.75 pt Monotype Dante
Typeset by Ellipsis Books Limited, Glasgow
Printed in England by Clays Ltd, St Ives plc

978-0-141-19454-7

www.greenpenguin.co.uk

Penguin Books is committed to a sustainable
future for our business, our readers and our
planet. This book is made from paper certified
by the Forest Stewardship Council.

Introduction

'It is with sadness and sorrow that we have carried out the mission entrusted to us by the constitutional President of the Republic. It has been an extremely arduous task, for we had to piece together a shadowy jigsaw, years after the events had taken place, when all the clues had been deliberately destroyed, all documentary evidence burned, and buildings demolished. The basis for our work has therefore been the statements made by relatives of those who had managed to escape from this hell, or even the testimonies of people who were involved in the repression but who, for whatever obscure motives, approached us to tell us what they knew.'

Ernesto Sábato, Prologue to 'Nunca Más', 1984

Ernesto Sábato is not only a central figure in the literary life of Argentina in the twentieth century, but in the political and civil life as well. In the dark days after the fall of the generals who had caused the disappearance of thousands of people and lost the Malvinas war, Sábato was chosen to chair the commission to investigate the crimes against human rights committed during their reign. As a novelist of immense seriousness and power, he was one of the few public figures who had moral authority and independence of mind in Argentina at that time. The commission gave its findings in September 1984 in a report entitled 'Nunca Más' ('Never Again'); it was detailed, horrifying and indisputable. As a result of what it disclosed the generals were put on trial. It was Sábato's report which established in the minds of people in Argentina the enormity of what had happened in their country.

Sábato was born in the province of Buenos Aires in 1911 and began his career as a scientist. In the early 1940s he was one of those many talented Argentines whose work appeared in the literary magazine *Sur*, edited by Victoria Ocampo. His first novel, *The Tunnel*, was published in the magazine in 1948. Although he knew and admired Borges and Bioy Casares and wrote about them in *Sur*, he was not an intimate of theirs; his early communism, for one thing, would not have endeared him to them. But he had something essential in common with them, and with other Argentine novelists such as Julio Cortázar and Juan José Saer; his work, especially the novels *The Tunnel*, *On Heroes and Tombs* (1961) and *The Angel of Darkness* (1974), was uncompromising and original both in tone and structure.

In his essay 'The Argentine Writer and Tradition' Borges made clear the scope and the scale of the ambition of the Argentine writers of the twentieth century. He suggested that by virtue of being so distant and so close to Europe at the same time the Argentine writer had more 'rights' to Western culture than anyone in any western nation. They were like Irish writers, he wrote, for whom it was 'enough, the fact of feeling Irish, different, to become innovators within English culture.' Thus Borges, Bioy Caseres and Sábato had in common the idea that it was not their role to explain Argentina to itself or to the world, it was not their job to explore changes in morals and manners in their country, or write social realism about Buenos Aires or the Pampas. Their job was not to remake their country in their own image, but remake literature itself, to offer it energy and fresh form.

Thus they took what was available from European literature and set about refining it or undermining it. In *The Tunnel*, Sábato took the idea of the demented male artist and the city, which had its roots in Russian and French fiction, and transported it to Buenos Aires, not to offer it local colour but to offer it instead further depth and strangeness. He created a hero even less heroic than usual and made his action even more inexplicable to everyone except himself. He allowed the surrounding existential darkness to be more even negative than normal; the protagonist's obsession became more driven and energetic and generally demented than that of his European counterparts, and also more oddly credible and intense.

The intensity and credibility arise from the style. Like Borges and Bioy, as *The Tunnel* makes clear, Sábato the scientist was interested in the clipped, declarative style of the murder mystery or the police file. While the novel describes extreme states of frenzied feeling and related activity, the prose is fiercely controlled; most of the sentences are short and describe a single action or emotion. Thus the distance between the subject of the novel and the tone of the prose offer a sort of tension to the narrative. This tension allows the narrator not to bother with analysis of motive, or flashbacks or character studies. It forces the reader to accept these as either totally unnecessary or fully understood.

The Tunnel is a novel about madness recollected in a prison cell; but it is not an apology for the madness or the actions which the madness caused, nor is it a rational explanation of them. Instead, it leads the reader into the demented world of the protagonist, using a deliberately calm style to suggest that this world is normal. The mind of Juan Pablo Castel is given a logic by the tone and sentence structure of the novel, which are precise and clear.

As in novels by Dostoyevsky and Kafka, there are moments when the rules governing despair are so closely undermined or re-examined or dramatised that the entire enterprise of living or thinking seems deeply absurd. What ensues is pure comedy. This happens, for example, in a classic scene in *The Tunnel* when Castel posts a letter to María and then decides he wishes to retrieve the letter. The encounter with the woman in the post office and the listing of regulations and demands put the reader on the side of Castel for a while. But not for long. The feeling that Castel is behaving both rationally and outrageously forces the reader to switch loyalty every few sentences; you feel one minute that Castel is a maniac and his own worst enemy and then the next minute you want him to retrieve the letter.

It is clear that *The Tunnel* belongs to a literary genre which explored dark areas of the self, and violence and irrationality in the anonymous mean streets of the modern city. It is important to remember that it is an Argentine novel only because it was open to European influences and contemporary genres which it set to develop and intensify. In its manic material and its grim laughter, it is not a metaphor for any society, Argentine or other-wise. But yet because of the style, so controlled and factual, and the content, which dealt with a world where violence, disorder and meglomania reigned, it is fascinating to read *The Tunnel* from

1948 in conjunction with the sober and detailed report which Sábato and his commission produced in 1984, about real murders committed in the real city where the fictional anti-hero Juan Pablo Castel once produced his art and where Sábato produced his first novel.

Colm Tóibín

I

It should be sufficient to say that I am Juan Pablo Castel, the painter who killed María Iribarne. I imagine that the trial is still in everyone's mind and that no further information about myself is necessary.

Granted, it is true that the devil himself cannot predict what people will remember, or why they remember it. I for one have never believed there is such a thing as a collective memory – which may be one way humans protect themselves. The phrase 'the good old days' does not mean that bad things happened less frequently in the past, only – fortunately – that people simply forget they happened. Obviously that view is not universally accepted. I, for example, would characterize myself as a person who prefers to remember the bad things. I might even argue for the past as 'the bad old days,' if it were not for the fact I consider the present as horrible as the past. I remember so many catastrophes, so many cynical and cruel faces, so many inhumane actions, that for me memory is a glaring light illuminating a sordid museum of shame. How often have I sat for hours in some dark corner of my studio, driven to despair by reading an account of some crime in the newspaper. Even so, it is not always in accounts of crimes that we find the most reprehensible acts of humankind; to a degree, criminals are the most decent and least offensive people among us. I do not make this statement because I myself killed another human being; it is my profound and honest conviction. Is a certain individual a menace to society? Then eliminate him and let that be an end to it. That is what I could call a *good deed*. Think how much worse it would be for society if that person were allowed to continue distilling his poison; think how pointless it would be if instead of eliminating him you attempted to forestall him by means of anonymous letters, or slander, or other loathsome measures. As for myself, I frankly confess that I now regret not having used my time to better advantage when I was a free man, that is, for not having done away with six or seven individuals I could name.

It is a terrible world; that truism demands no demonstration. Nonetheless, I will offer a single example as proof. Some years ago I read that in one of the concentration camps when a former pianist complained of hunger he was forced to eat a rat – a *live* rat.

However, that is not the subject I want to discuss now. If the opportunity arises, I will have more to say on the subject of the rat.

II

As I was saying, my name is Juan Pablo Castel. You may wonder what has motivated me to write this account of my crime (I may not have told you that I am going to relate all those details) and, especially, why I want to publish it. I know the human soul well enough to predict that some of you will believe it is from vanity. Think what you want, I don't give a damn. It has been a long time since I cared a fig for men's opinions *or* their justice. Go ahead, then, believe if you wish that I am publishing this story out of vanity. After all, I am made of flesh and blood and hair and fingernails like any other man, and I would consider it unrealistic for anyone to expect special qualities of me – particularly of me. There are times when a person feels he is a superman, until he realizes that he, too, is low, and vile, and treacherous. I do not need to comment on vanity. As far as I know, no human is devoid of this formidable motivation for Human Progress. People make me laugh when they talk about the modesty of an Einstein, or someone of his kind. My answer to them is that *it is easy to be modest when you are famous*. That is, *appear* to be modest. Even when you think a person hasn't the slightest trace of vanity, suddenly you discover it in its most subtle form: the vanity of modesty. How often we see that kind of person. Even a man like Christ – whether real or symbolic – a being for whom I have always felt, indeed, still do, the deepest reverence, spoke words that were motivated by vanity – or at least by arrogance. And what can you say of a Leon Bloy, who defended himself against the accusation of arrogance by arguing he had spent a lifetime serving people who did not deserve to lick his boots. Vanity is found in the most unlikely places: in combination with kindness, and selflessness, and generosity. When I was a boy I used to despair at the idea that my mother would die one day (as you grow older you learn that death is not only bearable but even comforting). I could not imagine that she might have faults. Now that she is dead, I can say that she was as good as a human being can ever be. But I remember in her last years, when I was a grown man, how at first it pained me to discover a very subtle trace of vanity or pride underlying her kindness and generosity. Something much more illustrative happened to me personally when she had an operation for cancer. In order to arrive in time I had to travel two full days without sleeping. When I reached her bedside, a tender smile lighted her face as she murmured a few words of sympathy (imagine, she was sympathizing with my fatigue!). And in the obscure depths of my being I felt the stirring of vain pride for having come so promptly. I confess this secret so that you will see I am sincere when I say that I am no better than any other man.

No, it is not because of vanity that I am telling this story. I might be willing to concede some degree of pride or arrogance. But why do I have this mania to explain everything that happens? When I began this account I had determined not to offer explanations of any kind. I wanted to tell the story of my crime:

that and nothing more. Anyone who was not interested did not have to read it. Although I would be very suspicious of that person, because it is precisely people who always demand explanations who are the most curious, and I am sure that none of them would miss the chance to read to the very end the story of a crime.

I could withhold the reasons that motivated me to write these confessional pages, but since I have no desire to be considered an eccentric, I will tell the truth, which is simple enough anyway: I thought that what I wrote might be read by a great many people now that I am a celebrity, and although I do not have many illusions about humanity in general and the readers of these pages in particular, I am animated by the faint hope that someone will understand me – *even if it is only one person.*

'Why,' someone will surely ask, 'such a faint hope if the book will be read by so many people?' This is typical of the kinds of questions I consider absolutely pointless; nevertheless, I must be prepared for them, because people constantly ask pointless questions, questions the most superficial analysis reveals to be unnecessary. I could speak until I dropped, yelling at the top of my lungs before an assembly of a hundred thousand Russians: not one would understand me. Do you see what I am saying?

There was one person who could have understood me. *But she was the very person I killed.*

III

Everyone knows that I killed María Iribarne Hunter. But no one knows how I met her, exactly what our relationship was, or why I came to believe I had to kill her. I will try to recount all this objectively. I may have suffered great pain because of María, but I am not stupid enough to claim that my behavior was exemplary.

In the annual spring art show I had exhibited a painting entitled *Motherhood*. It was painted in the style typical of many of my earlier works: as the critics say in their unbearable jargon, it was solid, soundly architectural. In short, it has all the qualities those charlatans always saw in my canvases, including a 'profoundly cerebral *je ne sais quoi.*' In the upper left-hand corner of the canvas was a remote scene framed in a tiny window: an empty beach and a solitary woman looking at the sea. She was staring into the distance as if expecting something, perhaps some faint and faraway summons. In my mind that scene suggested the most wistful and absolute loneliness.

No one seemed to notice the scene: their eyes passed over it as if it were something trivial, mere embellishment. With the exception of a single person, no one seemed to comprehend that the scene was an essential component of the painting. It was the day of the opening. A young woman I had never seen before stood for a long time before my painting, apparently ignoring the large figure of a woman in the foreground, a woman watching her child at play. Instead, she stared at the scene of the window, and as she did, I was sure that she was totally isolated from the world: she neither saw nor heard the people walking by or pausing to view my canvas.

I watched her nervously the whole time. Then she disappeared in the crowd, while I struggled between a crippling fear and an agonizing desire to call to her. Fear? Of what? Perhaps the same fear you feel when you bet every penny you own on one spin of the wheel. After she was gone I felt irritable, miserable; I was convinced I would never see her again now that she was lost among the millions of anonymous inhabitants of Buenos Aires.

I went home that night feeling nervous, discontent, dejected.

I went back every day until the show closed, stationing myself close enough to see everyone who stopped before my painting. But she never returned.

Throughout the months that followed I thought only of her and of the possibility that I might see her again. And in a way I painted only for her. It was as if the tiny scene of the window had begun to expand, to swallow up that canvas and all the rest of my work.

IV

Then one afternoon, finally, I saw her again. She was walking briskly down the opposite side of the street, like someone who must reach a specific place at a specific time.

I recognized her immediately; I could have picked her out of any crowd. I was filled with indescribable emotion. I had thought about her for so many months, imagined so many things, that when I saw her I did not know what to do.

In fact I had often thought about this moment, planning in minute detail what I would do in the event I met her. I think I have said that I am very shy; that is why I had thought and thought about a chance meeting, and about how to take advantage of it. The greatest difficulty in such imagined meetings is how to begin a conversation. I know a lot of men who have no difficulty in striking up a conversation with a strange woman. I confess that at one time I envied them greatly, because, although I was never a womanizer – or perhaps precisely for that reason – there were times I regretted not being able to communicate with a woman, that is, on those rare occasions when it seems impossible to accept the idea that she will never be a part of your life. Unfortunately, I was condemned never to be part of any woman's life.

In those imagined meetings I had analyzed several possibilities. I know the kind of person I am, and I know that because of my confusion and shyness I am totally lost in any unexpected or unplanned situation. As a result, I had prepared a number of logical, or at least possible, courses of action. (It is not *logical* that a close friend would send you an insulting anonymous letter, but we all know it is *possible*.)

The girl, I could assume, was in the habit of visiting art exhibits. If I saw her there, I could stop beside her and, without too much awkwardness, start a conversation about one of the paintings.

After examining this possibility in detail, I abandoned it. *I never go to art exhibits*. For a painter, this may seem a bizarre attitude, but there is a logical explanation, and I am sure that if I decide to give it, everyone will agree that I am right. Well, I may exaggerate when I say 'everyone.' No, I *know* I exaggerate. Experience has taught me that what seems clear and evident to me is never so to my fellow human beings. I have been burned so many times that now before I justify or explain anything, I mull it over a very long time; almost inevitably, I end up withdrawing into myself and not opening my mouth at all. That is why until today I had not decided to tell the story of my crime. Even at this moment, I still do not know whether it is worth the effort to try to explain this quirk of mine about art exhibits; I am afraid, however, that if I do not explain you will think that it is some kind of phobia, when in fact I have a very sound reason for my reluctance.

Actually, in this case there is more than one reason. Before I go on, I should say that I detest sects, brotherhoods, guilds, groups in general, any assemblage of morons congregating for reasons of profession, tastes, or similar manias. All these cliques have numbers of grotesque characteristics in common: repetition of type, their jargon, their arrogant conviction that they are better than everyone else.

I can see that I am complicating the problem, but I see no way to simplify it. Besides, anyone who wants to stop reading this account may do so now. He should know immediately that he has my unqualified permission.

What do I mean when I say 'repetition of type'? You have undoubtedly noticed how disagreeable it is to be with someone who has a tic in one eye, or whose lip is constantly twitching. Well, can you imagine a club of such people? Such extreme examples are not necessary, however. Merely think of a large family, in which certain traits, certain gestures, certain intonations of voice, are commonplace. I once had the experience of falling in love with a woman (without, of course, declaring it) and then fleeing in terror when faced with meeting her sisters. And something truly horrendous happened to me on a different occasion. I had admired certain traits in a woman I knew, but when I met one of her sisters I was depressed and ashamed for days: the very traits I had found so desirable seemed exaggerated and distorted in the sister, slightly caricatured, but not greatly. If they had been greatly exaggerated they would have been *different traits*, while in fact they were magnified just enough to seem ridiculous. The vaguely distorted vision of the first woman that I saw in her sister, besides the impression I described, made me feel ashamed, as if in some way I were partly to blame for the slightly ridiculous view I now had of the woman I had so admired.

Perhaps I see these things because I am a painter. I have

noticed that other people seem oblivious of family peculiarities. I should add that I have a similar reaction to painters who imitate great masters, those miserable daubers who paint in the manner of Picasso, for example.

Then there is the jargon, another of their characteristics that I cannot tolerate. Choose any example you like: psychoanalysis, communism, fascism, journalism. I have no favorites; I find them all repugnant. I offer the first example that comes to mind: psychoanalysis. Dr. Prato is a very talented man, and I believed he was a friend, a true friend. I suffered a terrible disillusionment when people began to persecute me and he took the part of the swine who were doing it. But let's not go into *that*. One day, almost as soon as I arrived at his office, Prato told me he had to go out, and invited me to go with him.

'Where?' I asked.

'To a cocktail the Society is giving,' he replied.

'What Society?' I asked with veiled irony, because if there is anything that galls me, it is the way they all use the definite article: *the* Society, they say, when they mean the Society of Psychoanalysts; *the* Party, for the Communist Party; *the* Seventh, for Beethoven's Seventh Symphony.

Prato looked at me, mildly surprised, but I gazed back with absolute innocence.

'Why, the Society of Psychoanalysts, Castel,' he answered, drilling me with those penetrating eyes Freudians consider necessary to their profession, and also looking as if he were asking himself, 'What new kind of madness is this guy up to now?'

I remembered having read something about a meeting or symposium to be presided over by a Dr. Bernard, or Bertrand.

Certain that it was not that meeting, I asked him if that was where we were going. He glanced at me with a scornful smile.

'Those charlatans,' he commented. 'Ours is the only internationally recognized psychoanalytic society.'

He sat down again at his desk, shuffled through some papers in a drawer, and finally handed me a letter written in English. I looked at it for the sake of courtesy.

'I can't read English,' I explained.

'This is a letter from Chicago. It vouches for the fact that we are the only society of psychoanalysts in all Argentina.'

My face registered admiration and profound respect.

So we left the office and drove to the cocktail party, where we found a mob of people. Some I knew by name, like Dr. Goldenberg, who had recently made quite a name for himself: in the course of treating a female patient, they had both ended up in a mental institution. He had just been released. I observed him closely, but he seemed no worse than the others. In fact he may even have been more placid, perhaps the result of his recent seclusion. The way he praised my paintings, I knew that he despised them.

Everything was so elegant that I was embarrassed to be seen in my ancient suit with the baggy-kneed trousers. The source of my uneasiness was not the trousers, however, but something I could not define. It had reached a climax when a beautiful young lady offered me an hors d'oeuvre as she continued her discussion with a colleague over some unimaginable problem of anal masochism.

I tried to find a quiet corner, but it was impossible. The room was crammed with identical people interminably parroting identical conversations. I fled to the outside world, and when I saw ordinary people (a newspaper vendor, a young boy, someone's driver), it seemed unreal that such people were milling around in a nearby apartment.

More than any other, however, I detest groups of painters. Partly, of course, because painting is what I know best, and we all know that we have greater reason to detest the things we know well. But I have still another reason: THE CRITICS. They are a plague I have never understood. If I were a great surgeon, and some fellow who had never held a scalpel in his hand, who was not a doctor, and who had never so much as put a splint on a cat's paw, tried to point out where I had gone wrong in my operation, what would people think? It is the same with painting. What is amazing is that people do not realize it is the same, and although they would laugh at the pretensions of the man who criticizes the surgeon, they listen with nauseating respect to the charlatans who comment on art. There might be some excuse for listening to the opinions of a critic who once painted, even if only mediocre works. But that is just as absurd; because what could be reasonable about a mediocre painter giving advice to a good one?

V

I have strayed from my subject. That is the result of this damned
compulsion to justify everything I do. Why the hell should I
explain why I do not go to art exhibits? It seems to me that every
person has a right to go or not to go, whatever he pleases,
without having to sign an affidavit of his reasons. Otherwise,
how far might such a mania lead? Well, enough of that, although
there is still a great deal I could say about art galleries: the
gossiping colleagues, the public's blindness, the imbecility of
those in charge of the hall and hanging the paintings. Fortunately
(or unfortunately) that kind of thing no longer interests me. If
it did, I might write a long essay entitled 'On the Manner
in Which the Painter May Defend Himself from the Friends
of Painting.'

At any rate, I had to eliminate the possibility of finding the
girl at an art exhibit.

On the other hand, she might have a friend who was also a
friend of mine. In that case a simple introduction would do.
Blinded by the painful glare of my shyness, I leapt at that
possibility. A simple introduction! How easy that would make
everything, how pleasant! My blindness prevented me from
seeing at once the basic flaw in the idea, that finding one of her

friends would be as difficult as finding her, because how could I find her friend if I did not know who she was? And if I knew who she was, why would I seek out a third party? There remained, it is true, the minor advantage of the introduction, which was not to be disdained. But clearly the first order of business was to find her, and *then* look for a common friend to introduce us.

Or I would take the opposite approach: to see if by chance any of my friends was a friend of hers. That I could do without having to find her first. All I had to do was ask each of my acquaintances whether they knew a young woman of such and such a height, with hair of such and such a color. However, this plan seemed too frivolous, and I rejected it. I was deterred by the mere idea of posing such a question to someone like Mapelli or Lartigue.

I want to make it clear that I did not discard this plan because it was unrealistic, but for the reasons I have just stated. There may be those who think it unlikely that an acquaintance of mine might also know her. It might seem this way to a superficial mind, but not to anyone in the habit of reflecting on human nature. There are in our society *horizontal strata* formed of persons with similar tastes, and within those strata, casual meetings (are there such things?) are not unusual, especially when the cause of the stratification is a quality common to a very few. I have had the experience of running into a person in Berlin, then in a remote village in Italy, and finally in a bookstore in Buenos Aires. Is it reasonable to attribute those repeated meetings to chance? But I am belaboring the obvious: any person devoted to music, or Esperanto, or spiritism, will know that.

I was forced, then, to fall back on the possibility I dreaded most: a chance meeting on the street. How the hell is it that some men manage to stop a woman and start a conversation with her, even an affair? I rejected out of hand any sequence of events in which I had to make the overtures: my ignorance of the stranger-in-the-street approach, and my looks, forced me to that sad but unshakable decision.

That left nothing but hope for a lucky break, one of those flukes that happens about once in a blue moon: that she would be the first to speak. So my happiness was tied to a one-in-a-million lottery I had to win to earn the right to play a second time, and in which I would receive the prize only on the wild shot I won a second day. In short, my only hope was that we might meet by chance, followed by the almost total improbability that she would speak first. I felt a kind of vertigo, a mixture of sadness and despair. Nevertheless, I began to lay my plans.

I envisioned scenes in which she spoke to me – for example, to ask about an address, or where to catch a bus – and from that opening, during months of reflection and melancholy, of rage, of abandon and hope, I constructed an endless series of variations. In one I was talkative, witty (something in fact I never am); in another I was taciturn; in still another, sunny and smiling. At times, though it seems incredible, I answered rudely, even with ill-concealed rage. It happened (in some of these imaginary meetings) that our exchange broke off abruptly because of an absurd irritability on my part, or because I rebuked her, almost crudely, for some comment I found pointless or ill-thought-out. I felt bitter after these frustrated encounters, and for several days I would reproach myself for the clumsiness that had caused me to lose my one opportunity to establish a relationship with her.

Fortunately, I would realize finally that everything was only imaginary, and that the actual possibility still existed. Then I would return to my preparations with renewed enthusiasm, imagining new and more fruitful dialogues on some street corner. In general, the greatest difficulty lay in linking her question with something as broad and foreign to her daily concerns as the general nature of art or, at least, her reactions to the scene of the window. Naturally, if you have time and tranquil surroundings, it is always possible to establish that kind of linkage logically; in a social gathering there is more than enough time, and in a certain way you expect to make that leap between totally unrelated subjects. But in the hustle and bustle of a Buenos Aires street, with people sweeping you along as they run to catch a bus, I would have to forfeit the luxury of that kind of conversation. On the other hand, if I cared about my future happiness, I could not forfeit it. So once again I would invent dialogues, the most concise and direct I could devise, that would lead from the sentence 'Where is the main post office?' to a discussion of various problems of expressionism or surrealism. It was not an easy task.

One insomnia-racked night I came to the conclusion that it was pointless and artificial to attempt this kind of conversation and that it would be best to strike boldly to the heart of the matter with a single question, playing everything on one number. For example, ask, 'Why did you look only at the window?' It is not unusual during nights of insomnia to act more decisively than during the daylight hours. The next morning, dispassionately analyzing the new possibility, I decided that I would never find the courage to ask that question point-blank. As always, discouragement drove me to the opposite extreme. I concocted a question so oblique that to reach the point that interested me (the window) would require a lengthy friendship: a question more or less on the order of 'Do you like art?'

I cannot remember now all the variations I invented. I remember only that some were so complex that they were useless in practical terms. Chances were nil that fate would offer me an intricate key to a lock of unknown design. It also happened that after examining so many elaborate variations I would forget the sequence of questions and answers, or confuse them, as can happen in chess plays when you imagine a match in your mind. As a result, I often transposed a sentence from one plan to a different one, with truly ridiculous and depressing results. For example, stopping to give her directions, and immediately asking, 'What do you think about art?' It was grotesque.

When I reached that point I took a brief holiday from shuffling combinations.

VI

When I saw her walking down the opposite side of the street, all the variations blended into one great jumble. A muddle of sentences I had contrived and memorized in my long preparatory gymnastics swam in my brain. 'Do you like art?' 'Why did you look only at the small window?' and a dozen others. Most insistent of all arose a question I had rejected as uncouth, one that made me blush, and feel even more ridiculous: 'Do you like Castel?'

These sentences, individually and in combination, formed a confused, constantly shifting jigsaw puzzle, until I realized that it was pointless to worry about what to say; I remembered that it was she who would have to take the initiative in any conversation. From that moment I felt idiotically calm. I think the thought even crossed my mind – also idiotically – 'Now we'll see how she manages to pull it off.'

Meanwhile, and in spite of my rationalizations, I felt so nervous and distraught that I could think of nothing to do but follow her progress down the opposite sidewalk, completely overlooking the fact that if I wanted to offer her the hypothetical opportunity to ask me about me about an address, I would have to cross the street and make myself available. Could there be anything more grotesque than to expect her to shout across the street to ask how to get somewhere?

What should I do? How long before I would have to make a move? I felt unutterably awkward. We continued this way for several blocks, she still walking purposefully.

I was depressed, but I had to follow through to the end: it was unthinkable that after waiting months for this moment I would let the opportunity slip away. Walking so rapidly while my mind was in such a whirl produced a strange sensation: my thoughts were like a blind and clumsy worm being borne along in a speeding automobile.

At Calle San Martín she turned the corner, walked a few steps, and entered the offices of the T. Company. I realized I would have to react quickly, and I followed her inside, although I felt that in those seconds I was committing an unbalanced and monstrous act.

She was waiting for the elevator. No one else was in the lobby. Someone more audacious than I inside my body asked this incredibly inane question:

'Is this the T. Company building?'

A sign with letters several meters high and covering a large portion of the building's facade proclaimed that this was indeed the T. Company.

Nevertheless, she turned quite naturally and answered that it was. (Later, reflecting on my question and the naturalness and calmness of her answer, I came to the conclusion that you do not always see signs when they are that large; therefore, my question was not as hopelessly stupid as I had first thought.)

As soon as she saw who I was, she blushed so deeply that I knew she recognized me. A variation that had never occurred to me, yet one that was entirely logical, because my photograph frequently appeared in magazines and newspapers.

I was so overcome with emotion that all I could manage was a second blundering question. I asked abruptly:

'Why are you blushing?'

She blushed even more and was opening her mouth to reply when I blurted, now completely out of control:

'You're blushing because you recognize me. And you think this meeting is a coincidence, but it isn't. There are no coincidences. I have been thinking about you for months. Today I saw you on the street and followed you. I have something important to ask you, something about the small window, do you understand?'

She looked frightened.

'The small window?' she stammered. 'What small window?'

I felt my knees buckle beneath me. Was it possible she did not remember? Then the window had not been of the slightest importance to her; she had felt nothing more than casual curiosity. I felt grotesque. My head was whirling; everything I had thought and planned during all those months (including the present moment) was ridiculous beyond belief, another of my typical imaginings, as preposterous as the recreation of a dinosaur starting from a single broken vertebra.

The girl was near tears. I felt my world collapsing about me, with no shred of calm or hope to cling to. I found myself saying something that now I am embarrassed even to write:

'I see that I have been mistaken. Good afternoon.'

I rushed from the building; I walked, almost ran, not knowing what direction I chose. I was a block from the building when I heard a voice behind me calling:

'Wait, wait!'

It was she. She had followed me, not daring to stop me. But she had, and now did not know how to justify what she had done. In a low voice, she said:

'Forgive me, please ... Forgive my stupidity. I was startled ...'

Seconds before, the world had been a chaos of meaningless objects and beings. Now I felt it falling into place, obedient to logic and order. Mutely, I listened.

'I didn't realize you were asking about the scene in your painting,' she said tremulously.

Unconsciously, I seized her arm.

'Then you remember it?'

She stood a moment without speaking, staring at the ground. Then she said, slowly:

'It is never out of my mind.'

Then she did something very strange. She seemed to have regretted what she had said, because she turned abruptly and hurried away, almost running. After a surprised instant, I ran after her, until I realized what a ridiculous figure I cut. I looked all around, and then continued at a fast but more normal pace. This decision was determined by two factors. First, it was grotesque for a well-known man to be chasing down the street after a woman. Second, *it was not necessary*. The latter was primary: I could see her anytime, going in or out of the office. Why charge down the street like a madman? What mattered, what really mattered, was that she remembered the scene in the window: 'It is never out of my mind.' I was happy. I felt that I could accomplish anything, and my only regret was having lost control while waiting for the elevator, and then a second time, now, running after her like a lunatic when it was clear I could find her at her office anytime I wanted.

VII

'At her office!' I almost screamed, once again feeling the strength drain from my knees. And who said she worked in that building? Does everyone who goes in work there? The idea of losing her again for months, perhaps forever, made me dizzy, and without any thought for convention I began to run like a desperate man. Soon I was back at the entrance of the T. Company building, but she was nowhere to be seen. Had she taken the elevator? I considered asking the elevator man, but what could I say? By now many women could have ridden the elevator, and I would have to give him specific details. What would he think? For a while I walked indecisively back and forth in front of the building. Then I crossed to the other sidewalk and examined the facade of the building, heaven knows why. Perhaps with the vague hope of seeing the girl looking from one of the windows? It was lunacy to think that she might look out and wave to me or make some sign. All I saw were the enormous letters proclaiming T. COMPANY.

Judging by eye, I hazarded that the sign covered some twenty meters of the facade; this calculation increased my uneasiness. But I had no time to yield to that sentiment now; I would have plenty of time later to torture myself. For the moment I saw no solution but to go into the building. Dynamically, I strode into the building and stood waiting for the elevator to descend. But with every floor it passed I could feel my determination dwindling and, in inverse ratio, my habitual timidity growing by leaps and bounds. By the time the elevator door opened I was very clear about what I must do: *not utter a word*. In that case, why take the elevator at all? Because it would have been too conspicuous not to, when several people had seen me waiting. What would they think? The only solution was to take the elevator but hold to my decision *not to utter a word*: a goal easily achieved, since not speaking was more normal than speaking. No one has the obligation to say anything in an elevator, that is, unless he is a friend of the operator, in which case it is natural to chat about the weather or inquire about a sick child. But as I had no relation at all to the man, in fact, had never seen him until that moment, my decision not to open my mouth could not produce the slightest complication. That I was not the only passenger made what I planned even simpler: no one would notice me.

Calmly, I stepped into the elevator, and everything went as I had foreseen, without difficulty. Someone mentioned the humid weather to the operator, and this pleasantry increased my sense of well-being, because it confirmed my reasoning. I felt a moment's nervousness when I said 'eight,' but no one would have noticed unless he knew the plan I had in mind at that moment.

When we reached the eighth floor I saw that another passenger was getting off with me, which complicated things slightly. I walked very slowly down the hall, waiting until he went into one of the offices. Then I could breathe easily. I walked the length of the corridor a few times, paused at a window to look out on the panorama of Buenos Aires, then went back and rang for the elevator. In a few minutes I was again at the entrance to the building without any of the unpleasant scenes I had feared (unusual questions from the elevator operator, for example) having occurred. I lighted a cigarette. I still held the lighted match in my hand when I realized that my calm was absolutely absurd: it was true that nothing unpleasant had happened; it was equally true that *nothing at all had happened.* To be blunt, I had lost the girl, unless she worked in this office building. If she had come to run a simple errand, she could already have gone in and out without meeting me. 'Of course,' I rationalized, 'it's also possible that if she went to do an errand, she isn't through yet.' This thought gave me heart, and I decided to wait opposite the entrance.

For one hour I stood watching, without results. I analyzed the possibilities:

1. The errand was taking a long time; in that case I should continue to wait.

2. After what happened, she had been upset and decided to walk awhile before doing her errand; this also meant I must wait.

3. She worked here; in this case, I would have to wait until closing time.

'So if I wait until closing,' I reasoned, 'that will cover all three possibilities.'

This logic seemed ironclad, and I felt calm enough to wait comfortably in the sidewalk café on the corner; from there I could see anyone coming out. I ordered a beer and looked at my watch: it was three-fifteen.

The longer I waited the more sure I was of the last hypothesis: she worked there. At six I left my table; it seemed more prudent to wait at the entrance. Large numbers of people would be leaving at the same time and I might not be able to see her from the café.

A few minutes after six the employees began to leave.

By six-thirty nearly everyone had left – an inference made clear by the fact that as the minutes passed, fewer and fewer people came out. By six forty-five there was almost no one, only an occasional executive. Unless . . . She might be an executive ('Absurd,' I thought), or secretary to an executive ('That's it.' I felt a flicker of hope).

By seven it was all over.

VIII

Going home; I was deeply depressed, but I made an effort to think clearly. My brain is in constant ferment and, when I get nervous, ideas roil in a giddy ballet. In spite of that – perhaps because of it – I have learned to control my ideas and arrange them in strict order. If I could not do that, I think I would soon go mad.

As I said, I returned home in a state of deep depression, but that did not prevent me from filing and classifying ideas; for I knew I had to think clearly if I did not want to lose the only person who had understood my painting.

Either she had gone into the building to do an errand, or she worked there; there was no other possibility. Obviously, I preferred the latter hypothesis. If that were true, when she left me she had been upset and had decided to go home. I should wait for her the next day, then, across from the entrance.

I considered the second possibility: the errand. Upset by our chance meeting, she had returned home and postponed the errand until the next day. In this case, too, my best bet was to watch for her at the entrance.

These were the two acceptable possibilities. The third struck fear in my heart: she had completed her errand during the time

I was returning to the building, or during my adventure in the elevator. That is, we both had gone in and out, but not seen each other.

I had been only a while, and it was unlikely, although possible, that that was what had happened. The errand, for example, could have consisted of delivering a letter. Under those conditions, there was no point in going back the next day to wait for her.

Two of the possibilities were favorable, nevertheless, and I clung to them with desperation.

My mood by the time I reached my house was mixed. On the one hand, every time I thought of what she had said ('It is never out of my mind'), my heart thudded violently and I felt an obscure but vast and powerful panorama opening before me. I felt intuitively that a great force, dormant until that moment, was being unleashed within me. On the other hand, I suspected it might be a long time before I found her again. I must find her. I found myself repeating aloud, 'I must, I must!'

IX

Early the next morning I was standing across from the entrance to the T. building. The last of the employees entered the building, but she was not among them. Obviously she did not work there, although the slim chance remained that she was ill and had not come to work.

I had not eliminated the possibility of the errand, so I decided to spend the morning watching from the corner café.

I had lost all hope (it must have been about eleven-thirty) when I saw her coming out of the subway. Elated, I leapt to my feet and hurried toward her. When she saw me she stopped as if turned to stone; it was clear that she had not counted on such an apparition. It was curious, but the sense that my mind had worked with steely exactitude caused a surge of uncommon energy. I felt strong: I was possessed by manly decisiveness, ready for anything. I was so much in command that I grasped her arm almost brutally and without a word marched her along Calle San Martín toward the Plaza. She seemed devoid of will, and went along silently.

When we had gone a couple of blocks, she asked:

'Where are you taking me?'

'To Plaza San Martín. We have a lot to talk about,' I replied, walking resolutely ahead, still propelling her by the arm.

She murmured something about the T. building but I paid no attention, still pulling her along. I repeated:

'We have a lot to talk about.'

She offered no resistance. I felt like a raging river sweeping along a tree limb. When we reached the plaza I looked for an isolated bench.

'Why did you run away?' was my first question. She looked at me with the same expression I had noticed the day before when she said 'It is never out of my mind.' It was a strange look, unwavering, penetrating; it seemed to come from somewhere in the past. That look reminded me of something; I had seen those eyes before, but I couldn't remember where.

'I don't know,' she replied finally. 'I would like to leave now.'

I tightened my grip on her arm.

'Promise me you will never leave me again. I need you. I need you very much.'

Again she stared at me as if studying me, but said nothing. She fixed her eyes on a distant tree.

In profile, she did not remind me of anything. Her face was beautiful, but there was something hard in her expression. Her hair was long and chestnut-colored. Physically, she seemed not much more than twenty-six, but there was something about her that suggested age, something reminiscent of a person who has lived a long time. Not gray hair or any purely physical indication, but something undefined, surely spiritual. It may have been her expression, but how physical can an expression be? Was it something about her mouth? Because although the mouth and lips are physical, the way of holding them, even certain lines around them, are spiritual. I could not be sure at that moment, nor can I define now, what it was precisely that gave the impression of age. It may have been the way she spoke.

'I need you very much,' I repeated.

She did not reply, but continued to stare at the tree.

'Why don't you say something?' I asked.

Never taking her eyes from the tree, she answered:

'I'm nobody. You are a great artist. I don't see why you need me.'

I shouted, almost brutally:

'I tell you I need you! Don't you understand?'

Eyes still on the distant tree, she murmured:

'Why?'

I did not immediately reply. I dropped her arm and sat there thinking. In fact, why did I need her? Until that moment I had not asked myself that question, but merely obeyed a kind of instinct. With a small stick I began to trace geometric patterns in the dirt.

'I don't know,' I murmured after a long pause. 'I don't know yet.'

My mind was racing as I added more and more complex designs to the drawing.

'My mind is a dark labyrinth. Sometimes there are flashes, like lightning, that illuminate some of the passageways. I never know why I do certain things. No, that isn't right . . .'

I felt almost stupid. This was not at all like me. I made a concerted mental effort. Was I saying I was not a rational person? On the contrary, my mind is like a calculating machine, constantly computing. For example, in terms of what was happening that minute, hadn't I spent months reasoning and analyzing and classifying hypotheses? And, in a way, wasn't it my capacity for logical thought that had finally led me to María?

I felt I was getting close to the truth, very close, and I was afraid I would lose it. Again I made a concerted effort. I cried:

'It isn't that I don't reason things out. Just the opposite, my mind never stops. But think of the captain of a ship who is constantly charting his position, meticulously following a course toward an objective. But also imagine that *he does not know why he is sailing toward it*. Now do you understand?'

She glanced at me for an instant, bewildered, then again turned to stare at the tree.

'I feel that you are somehow essential to something I have to do, although I am not yet sure why.'

Again I doodled in the dirt with the stick as I continued to order my thoughts. After a few moments I added:

'For now, I know that it has something to do with the scene in the window: you were the only person who paid any attention to it.'

'I'm not an art critic,' she said softly.

That infuriated me, and I shouted:

'Don't mention those cretins to me!'

She turned, startled. I lowered my voice, and explained why I had no faith in art critics, my theory of the scalpel, and all that.

She listened, still not turning to look at me, and when I was through, she commented:

'You complain, but the critics have always praised you.'

I was indignant.

'Worse luck for me! Don't you understand? That is one of the things that has embittered me and convinced me I'm on the wrong track. Just remember what happened in that show. Not a single one of those charlatans appreciated the importance of that scene. There was only one person who saw how important it was – you. And you're not a critic. No, I'm wrong. There was one other person who reacted to the window, but negatively. He upbraided me for it. It made him apprehensive, he said, almost nauseated. In contrast, you . . .'

Eyes straight ahead, she said quietly:

'But . . . couldn't it be that . . . that I had the same opinion?'

'The same opinion?'

'The opinion the other person had.'

My nerves were raw. I strained to see her expression, but her face in profile was inscrutable, her jaw tightly clenched. I replied confidently:

'You think what I think.'

'And what is it you think?'

'I don't know. I can't answer that question, either. Maybe it would be better to say that you *feel* what I feel. You looked at that scene as I would have had I been in your place. I don't know what you think, I don't know what I think, but I know you think the way I do.'

'Does that mean you don't plan your paintings?'

'I used to plan every detail. I constructed them the way you construct a house. But not that scene. I felt I had to paint it that way, even though I didn't know why. And I still don't know why. The truth is that it doesn't have anything to do with the rest of the painting. I have to admit that one of those idiots pointed that out to me. I am groping my way in the dark, and I need your help because I know you feel the way I do.'

'I'm not exactly sure what you think.'

I was growing impatient. I replied curtly:

'Haven't I been telling you I don't know what I think? If I

could say in words what I feel, it would be almost the same as thinking clearly. Isn't that true?'

'Yes, that's true.'

Now I was silent. I was thinking, trying to see things clearly. Then I added:

'Maybe you could say that all my previous work was superficial.'

'What previous work?'

'The work before the window.'

I was concentrating, refining my thoughts.

'No, no, it isn't that. That isn't it. It isn't that my work was more superficial.'

What did I mean, in fact? Never, until that moment, had I put my mind to this problem. Now I was beginning to realize how close I had been to being a sleepwalker when I painted the scene of the window.

'No, it isn't that it was more superficial,' I repeated, as if thinking aloud. 'I don't know. All this has something to do with humankind in general, you know? I remember that just days before I painted it, I had read that a man in a concentration camp had asked for something to eat and they had forced him to eat a live rat. There are times I feel that nothing has meaning. On a tiny planet that has been racing toward oblivion for millions of years, we are born amid sorrow; we grow, we struggle, we grow ill, we suffer, we make others suffer, we cry out, we die, others die, and new beings are born to begin the senseless comedy all over again.'

Was that really it? I sat pondering the idea of the absence of meaning. Was our life nothing more than a sequence of anonymous screams in a desert of indifferent stars?

María had not commented.

'The scene on the beach frightens me,' I added, following this long silence. 'Although I know that it is something more profound than mere fear. No, I think what I'm trying to say is that it says something more profound about *me* . . . I mean . . . Now I think I've hit on the key. The message is still unclear, but it says something profound about *me*.'

I heard her say quietly:

'Maybe a message of despair?'

I peered at her anxiously.

'Yes,' I said. 'I think it *is* a message of despair. You see, you do think like me.'

She thought a moment, and asked:

'And do you think a message of despair is commendable?'

This was not a question I had expected.

'No,' I replied. 'I guess it isn't. What do you think?'

She sat for a palpably long moment without answering. Finally she turned and looked directly at me.

'The word *commendable* isn't relevant here,' she said, as if answering her own question. 'What is relevant is the truth.'

'And do you think the scene is truthful?' I asked.

She nodded, and said with an edge in her voice:

'I believe it is truthful.'

The hardness in her face and eyes disturbed me. 'Why is she so cold?' I asked myself. 'Why?' Perhaps she sensed my anxiety, my hunger to communicate, because for an instant her expression softened, and she seemed to offer a bridge between us. But I felt that it was a temporary and fragile bridge swaying high above an abyss. Her voice was different when she added:

'But I don't know what you will gain by seeing me. I hurt everyone who comes near me.'

X

We agreed we would meet soon. I was ashamed to tell her that I wanted to see her the very next day, that I wanted her to stay with me right then, that she must never leave me again. In spite of my astounding memory, I do have sudden inexplicable lapses. I do not know now what I said to her, but I remember her saying that it was time for her to go.

That same night I called her. A woman answered. When I told her I wanted to speak with Señorita María Iribarne she seemed to hesitate a second, but then said she would see if she was in. Almost immediately I heard María's voice, but her formal, businesslike tone gave me a start.

'I must see you, María,' I said. 'I've been thinking about you constantly, every second since I left you.'

I paused, trembling. She did not answer.

'Why don't you say something?' I asked, growing increasingly nervous.

'Wait a minute,' she said.

I heard her put down the receiver. Then after a few seconds I heard her voice again; now it was her true voice. She sounded as if she was trembling, too.

'I couldn't talk,' she explained.

'Why?'

'There are a lot of people around.'

'Then how can you talk now?'

'Because I closed the door. When I close the door they know I am not to be disturbed.'

'I must see you, María.' My voice was harsh. 'Since I left you at noon I've done nothing but think of you.'

No reply.

'Why don't you answer me?'

'Castel,' she began hesitantly.

I shouted at her, indignant. 'Don't call me Castel!'

Then, timidly, 'Juan Pablo . . .'

I felt that those two words were the beginning of infinite happiness.

But María had stopped again.

'What's happening?' I asked. 'Why don't you say something?'

'So have I,' she half whispered.

'So have you *what*?' I insisted.

'So have I, been thinking of nothing else.'

'What do you mean, nothing else,' I asked. I was insatiable.

'About everything.'

'What do you mean, everything? Tell me. *What*?'

'Oh, how strange all this is . . . your painting . . . our meeting yesterday . . . and today . . . I don't know . . .'

Imprecision has always irritated me.

'Look! I told you that I have done nothing but think of you,' I said. 'But you didn't say you've thought about me.'

A long moment. Then she said:

'I told you, I've been thinking about *everything*.'

'But what? I want you to tell me in detail.'

'But it's all so strange, it's all been so strange ... I find it disturbing. Of course I thought about you.'

My heart lurched. But I needed details. I thrive on details, not generalities.

'But how, *how*?' I was more and more agitated. 'I've thought of everything about you. About your profile when you were staring at the tree, about your chestnut hair, about how hard your eyes were and then how suddenly your expression softened, about the way you walk—'

'I have to hang up,' she interrupted. 'Someone is coming.'

Desperately, I managed to say, 'I'll call you tomorrow, early.'

'All right' was her abrupt reply.

XI

I spent a restless night. I couldn't sketch, I couldn't paint, although I tried many times to start on something. I went out for a walk and suddenly found myself on Calle Corrientes. Something very strange was happening: I was seeing the world through sympathetic eyes. I think I remember saying that I intended to be absolutely impartial in telling this story, and now I am going to offer the first proof of that by confessing one of my worst faults. I have always looked on people with antipathy, even revulsion – especially crowds of people. I have always despised the beach in summer, soccer games, the races, demonstrations. I have felt affection for a few men, and an occasional woman; for some I have felt admiration (I am not an envious man), for others, true sympathy. I have always had tenderness and compassion for children (especially when through supreme mental effort I have tried to forget that one day they will be adults like anyone else). *In general*, however, humankind has always seemed detestable. I do not mind telling you that there have been times after I observed a particular character trait that I could not eat for a day, or paint for a week. It is incredible to what degree greed, envy, petulance, vulgarity, avarice – in short, the entire spectrum of traits that compose our miserable condition – can be revealed in a face, in a way of walking, in a look. It seems only natural that after such an encounter a person would not want to eat or paint – even live. Nonetheless, I want to make it clear that I take no pride in this trait. I know it is a sign of pride, and I also know that greed and petulance and avarice and vulgarity have often found a welcome spot in my heart. But I said that I would tell this story with complete impartiality, and that is what I intend to do.

That night my scorn for humanity seemed nullified, or at least temporarily absent. I went to the café Marzotto. I suppose you know that people go there to listen to tangos, but to listen to them the way a true believer listens to Bach's *Saint Matthew Passion*.

XII

About ten the next morning I called María. The same woman answered the telephone. When I asked for Señorita María Iribarne, she told me she had left that morning for the country. I was stunned.

'For the country?' I repeated.

'Yes, sir. Are you Señor Castel?'

'Yes, I am Castel.'

'She left a letter for you. She said to say she was sorry, but she didn't have your address.'

I had counted so strongly on the idea of seeing her that day, and had hoped for such momentous results from the meeting, that this news left me totally deflated. A series of questions rushed through my mind. Why had she decided to go to the country? Evidently she had made this decision following our telephone conversation because, if not, she would have said something about a trip to the country, and certainly she would not have agreed to talk to me the next morning. But if her decision was subsequent to the telephone conversation, was it also a *consequence of that conversation*? And if so, why? Was she running away from me again? Was she afraid that we would meet accidentally, as before?

This unexpected trip to the country awakened my first doubts. As always, I began to recall suspicious details I had ignored at the time. Why the change of voice the day before on the telephone? Who were the 'people' who were 'around' and who prevented her from speaking normally? Furthermore, the change of voice *proved she was capable of pretense.* And why had the maid hesitated when I asked for Señorita Iribarne? But more than any other, one sentence kept eating into my brain like acid: 'When I close the door they know I am not to be disturbed.' I realized that there were dark shadows around María.

These thoughts were forming in my mind as I hurried toward her house. It was strange that she had not found my address. By contrast, I already knew both her address and her telephone number. She lived on Calle Posadas, almost at the corner of Seaver.

By the time I reached the fifth floor and rang the bell, I was shaking with emotion.

The door was opened by a servant who seemed to be Polish, or some such nationality, and when I gave him my name, he led me to a study filled with books. Bookshelves lined the walls to the ceiling, but books were also piled on the two small tables, and even one of the chairs. I was struck by the abnormal size of many of the volumes.

I had got up to take a closer look around the library when suddenly I had the sensation that someone behind my back was silently watching me. I turned and saw a man at the opposite end of the room. He was tall and thin, with a handsome head. He smiled in my direction, but only in my *general direction.* Though his eyes were wide open, I realized he could not see. That explained the unusually large books.

'You are Castel, right?' he said cordially, extending his hand toward me.

'Yes, Señor Iribarne,' I replied, taking the proferred hand. I was bewildered; I wondered what his relationship to María might be.

As he motioned me to a chair, he smiled with slight irony. 'My name is not Iribarne, and you must not call me Señor. I am Allende, María's husband.'

Accustomed to appraising, and perhaps interpreting, silences, he immediately added:

'María always uses her maiden name.'

I stood frozen as a statue.

'María has told me a lot about your painting. Since I became blind fairly late in my life, I can still envision things rather well.'

It was as if he were apologizing for his blindness. I did not know what to say. All I wanted was to be alone, out of this room, somewhere I could digest this new information!

He removed a letter from a pocket and handed it to me.

'Here is your letter,' he said simply, as if there were nothing extraordinary about his delivering a letter to me.

I took the letter and started to put it in my pocket, but the blind man added, as if he had seen what I was doing:

'Go ahead, read it. Although, since it's from María, it can't be very urgent.'

I was trembling. As he lighted a cigarette – after offering one to me – I tore open the envelope. I removed the letter. It consisted of a single sentence:

I think of you, too.
María

When Allende heard me folding the sheet of paper, he asked:

'Nothing urgent, I imagine.'

Making a supreme effort, I replied:

'No, nothing urgent.'

I felt like some kind of monster when I saw the blind man smile, gazing toward me with wide open eyes.

'That's just like María,' he said, as if thinking aloud. 'People often mistake María's impulses for urgent need. She does things spontaneously, but without changing very much of anything. How can I explain it to you?'

He gazed abstractedly toward the floor, as if seeking a clearer explanation there. After a moment, he said:

'As if someone stranded in a desert suddenly moved with great speed to a different location. You understand? The speed is really unimportant; the person is still in the same desert.'

He smoked and meditated a moment longer, as if I were not there. Then he added:

'Although I'm not sure that's exactly it. I don't have a gift for metaphor.'

I could not think how to escape from that damned room. The blind man seemed to be in no hurry at all. 'What kind of ridiculous farce is this?' I asked myself.

'Today, for example,' Allende continued. 'She gets up at dawn and tells me she's going out to the *estancia*.'

'To the *estancia*?' I repeated hazily.

'Yes, our *estancia*. I mean, it was my grandfather's, but now it's in the hands of my cousin Hunter. I suppose you know him?'

This new revelation added to my anxiety, and also made me peevish. What could María possibly see in that womanizing, cynical imbecile? I made an effort to be calm, reassuring myself that she had not gone to the *estancia* to be with Hunter, but because she liked the solitude of the country and because it was the family estate. Nevertheless, my heart sank.

'I know who he is,' I said bitterly.

Before the blind man could reply, I added unceremoniously: 'I must go.'

'Oh, no. I'm sorry to hear that,' Allende remarked. 'I hope we will be seeing each other again.'

'Yes, yes, of course,' I answered.

He walked me to the door. We shook hands and I fled. As the elevator was descending, I repeated with rage: 'What kind of ridiculous farce is this!'

XIII

I needed to clear my mind, to think calmly. I walked down Posadas toward one of the parks near La Recoleta cemetery.

My brain was in pandemonium: swarming ideas, emotions of love and loathing, questions, resentment, and memories all blended together or flashed by in rapid succession.

What, for example, could she have had in mind by having me come to her house to pick up a letter and then have her husband deliver it to me? And why hadn't she warned me she was married? And what the hell was she doing at the *estancia* with that bastard Hunter? And why hadn't she waited until I called? And that blind man, what kind of character was he? I have already said that I have a miserable opinion of human beings. Now I must confess that *I do not like blind people at all*, and in their presence I have the same feeling I get when I see certain cold, clammy, voiceless creatures like snakes. If you add to that the effect of reading in front of him a letter from his wife that said 'I think of you, too,' it will not be difficult to imagine the revulsion I felt at that moment.

I tried to create a little order from the chaos of my ideas and emotions, and to proceed methodically, as was my custom. I would have to begin at the beginning, and the beginning (at least the immediate beginning) was, obviously, the telephone conversation. There was more than one foggy detail about that conversation.

In the first place, if it was the normal thing in that household for María to have relationships with men – as proved by the letter her husband had delivered – then why use a neutral tone of voice until the door was closed? Then, what was the meaning of her comment 'When I close the door they know I am not to be disturbed'? Apparently it meant she often closed the door to talk on the telephone. But it was not likely she would close the door for trivial conversations with family friends: the reasonable deduction was that it was to have conversations like ours. But that meant there were others like myself in her life. How many? And who?

My first thought was Hunter, but I ruled him out immediately. Why talk to him by telephone if she could see him at the *estancia* anytime she wanted? In that case, who were the others?

Surely that exhausted the question of the telephone conversation. But no, that was not the end of it. There was still the problem of her answer to my explicit question. I recalled with bitterness that when I had asked her whether she had thought of me, she had said only, after much stalling: 'I told you, I've been thinking about *everything*.' You do not commit yourself by answering a question with such a reply. After all, the proof that her answer was vague was that she herself, the next day (or that same night) had thought it necessary to reply in very precise terms in a letter.

'So,' I said to myself, 'let's turn to the letter.' I took it from my pocket, and reread the brief message.

I think of you, too.
María

The handwriting indicated she had been nervous or, if not, that it was the handwriting of a nervous person. These are not the same things, however, because if it is the former, the handwriting betrayed real emotion, which would be a good omen for me. Whichever it was, I was exuberant about the signature: *María*. Simply, *María*. Such simplicity gave me a vague feeling of possession, a vague sense that the girl was now a part of my life and that, in a certain way, she now belonged to me.

Oh, God! My moments of happiness are so fleeting . . . That impression, as a case in point, could not withstand the feeblest analysis. Did I think that her husband didn't call her María? And surely Hunter called her that, too. What else would he call her? And all the others she talked to behind closed doors? Certainly no one she spoke to behind closed doors was going to address her respectfully as 'Señorita Iribarne.'

Señorita Iribarne! Now I understood the maid's hesitation the first time I called. How embarrassing! When I examined it logically, it was further proof that this kind of call was not a novelty. Obviously, the first time someone asked for 'Señorita Iribarne' the surprised maid had automatically corrected the caller, underlining the 'Señora.' But after it happened several times, she must have shrugged her shoulders and decided not to bother anymore. She had hesitated when I called – that was natural. But she had not corrected me.

When I reconsidered the letter, I decided there was room for any number of deductions. I began with what was most extraordinary: the way the letter was delivered. I remembered the excuse the maid had conveyed: 'She said to say she was sorry, but she didn't have your address.' It was true: she hadn't asked me my address, nor had it occurred to me to give it to her. But in her place, the first thing I would have done was look it up in the telephone directory. It was too much to believe that she was simply too lazy; the conclusion was unavoidable: *María wanted me to come to the house and wanted me to meet her husband face-to-face.* But why? At this point, matters became even more complex. One possibility was that María enjoyed using her husband as a go-between. Conversely, it might be the husband who received the pleasure. It might be both. In addition to the pathological explanations, there was one normal possibility: María wanted me to know she was married so I would see why we should not go on.

I am sure that many of you reading these pages will favor the third hypothesis, and conclude that only a man like myself could choose one of the other two. During the time in my life when I had friends, they often laughed at my passion for always selecting the most tortuous route. I ask myself, though, *why reality has to be simple.* Experience has taught me just the opposite; it almost never is simple, and when something seems unusually clear, when some action appears to obey a simple logic, there are usually complex motives behind it. A simple example. People who donate to charities are generally con-sidered to be better, more generous, than those who do not. I have enormous contempt for this simplistic notion. Anyone knows that you do not solve the problems of a beggar (an authentic beggar) with a dime or a crust of bread. All it does is solve the psychological problems of the man buying a reputation and peace of mind for practically nothing. Judge for yourself just how niggardly people are when they are not willing to spend more than a few cents a day to assure peace of mind and gain a self-congratulatory sense of their own beneficence. How much greater purity of spirit and courage are required to bear the burden of human misery without this hypocritical (and penny-pinching) practice.

But I want to get back to the letter.

Only a simpleminded person could defend the third hypothesis, because it crumbles at the most cursory examination. 'María wanted me to know she was married so I would see why we should not go on.' Beautiful. But in that case, why did she resort to such a cumbersome and cruel course of action? Couldn't she have told me personally, even by telephone? Couldn't she have written me, if she lacked the nerve to tell me? There was an even more convincing argument: If she wanted me to know, why didn't the *letter* say she was married – which I could see for myself; why didn't it beg me to be satisfied with a less personal friendship? No, my friends. To the contrary, the letter was a letter intended to cement our relationship, to fan the fires, and to lead us down the most dangerous path.

That left the pathological hypotheses. Was it possible that María enjoyed using Allende as her go-between? Was he the one who sought these opportunities? Or had fate amused itself by uniting those two?

I was suddenly horrified at the lengths I had gone to in my compulsion to analyze every action and every word. I remembered María staring at the tree in the plaza and listening as I poured out my thoughts to her. I remembered her timidity, how she had fled from me. I was filled with an infinite tenderness. She seemed fragile to me, an unreal child in a cruel world of ugliness and misery. I felt what I had so often felt from the first moment in the art gallery: *that she was like me.*

I forgot all my sterile reasoning, my savage deductions. I indulged myself by picturing her face, her expression – that expression that reminded me of something I could not identify – her profound and melancholy way of thinking. I felt that the unfocused love I had nourished through so many years of loneliness had crystallized in María. How could I think such absurd things about her?

I tried to forget all my moronic deductions about the telephone, about the letter, the *estancia*, Hunter.

But I could not.

XIV

The days that followed were frantic. In my haste, I had not asked when María would be returning from the *estancia*. That same day I called to ask about her return. The maid told me she did not know. I asked her for María's address at the *estancia*.

That night I wrote a desperate letter, asking María when she was coming home, and begging her to call me as soon as she was back in Buenos Aires – or at least to write. I took the letter to the main post office and sent it by registered mail, to minimize the risk.

As I said, I spent some frantic days, and a thousand times the dark thoughts that had tormented me since my visit to Calle Posadas raced through my mind. I had this dream. One night I went to a lonely old house. It was a house that somehow I had known and infinitely desired since my childhood, so that when I went inside, I was guided by old memories. But at times I found myself lost in the darkness, or I had the impression that enemies lurking behind my back were about to attack me, or that people were whispering about me and making fun of me, of my naïveté. Who were those people, and what did they want? And yet, in spite of everything, I felt that my first adolescent loves were being reborn in the house, with the same trembling and sensations of sweet madness and fear and joy. When I awoke, I realized that the house in the dream was María.

XV

In the days that preceded the arrival of her letter, my thoughts were like an explorer lost in a misty landscape: here and there, straining my eyes, I could glimpse vague silhouettes of people and objects, blurred outlines of perils and chasms. When the letter came, it was as if the sun had come out.

But this was a black sun, a nocturnal sun. I do not know whether you can say that, but although I am not a writer and although I am not sure whether it is correct, I will not withdraw the word *nocturnal*. Of all the words that make up our imperfect language, *nocturnal* was perhaps the most appropriate for María.

This is the letter:

> *I have spent three strange days: the sea, the beach, the paths keep bringing me memories of other days. Not merely images, voices as well, shouts and long silences from other times. It is curious, but life is a process of constructing future memories; at this very moment, here where I sit facing the sea, I know that I am creating memories that one day will bring me melancholy and despair.*
>
> *The sea lies before me, eternal and raging. My weeping from that other time is futile; futile, too, my waiting on the*

*lonely beach, gazing unblinkingly at the sea. Did you some-
how divine my memory, or did you paint the memory of many
people like us?*

*But now your figure is interposed; you stand between me
and the sea. My eyes meet your eyes. You are quiet, faintly
sad. You are looking at me as if asking for my help.*
María

How well I understood her; what miraculous emotions welled
up in my heart when I read this letter! There was such a tangible
intimacy in her words that I was sure María was mine. Mine
alone. 'You stand between me and the sea.' There was no other
person; we two were alone, as I had known intuitively the
moment she looked at the scene of the window. In fact, how
could we be other than intimate when we had known each other
for a thousand years, for all time? When she paused before my
painting and looked at that small scene, not hearing or seeing
the crowd around us, it was as if we were already on intimate
terms, as if I already knew the person she was, how much I
needed her, and how she, too, needed me.

Oh, God! And yet I killed you! It was *I* who killed you, I, who
saw you mute and anxious, but could not touch you through
the wall of glass. I, so stupid, so blind, so incredibly selfish and
cruel!

Well, that's enough of that. I said I would tell this story in a
straightforward way, and I will.

XVI

I was desperately in love with María, and yet the word love had never been spoken between us. I could scarcely wait for her return from the *estancia* to say it to her.

But she did not return. And as the days went by, a kind of madness was growing within me. I wrote her a second letter that said merely, 'I love you, María, I love you, I love you!'

After two days, an eternity, I received an answer containing only these words: 'I am afraid I will bring you great harm.' I answered that instant. 'I don't care what you do to me. If I couldn't love you, I would die. Every second I spend without seeing you is torture.'

Day after horrible day went by, but no answer came. Desperate, I wrote: 'You are tearing me apart.'

The next day the phone rang and, distantly, I heard her faltering voice.

Except for the word *María*, which I repeated incessantly, I could not think what to say. It would have been impossible, anyway; my throat was so tight I couldn't speak clearly. María said:

'I am coming back to Buenos Aires tomorrow. I will call you as soon as I get there.'

The next afternoon she called me from her house.

'I must see you,' I said. 'Now.'

'All right. I'll meet you today,' she replied.

'I'll be waiting in the Plaza San Martín.'

María seemed to hesitate. 'I prefer La Recoleta. I'll be there at eight.'

How I had waited for that moment. I wandered aimlessly through the streets to make the time pass more quickly. What tenderness filled my heart. How beautiful the world seemed, the summer afternoon, the children playing on the sidewalks. Today I can reflect on how we are blinded by love; how magically love transforms reality. The world, beautiful? What a laugh!

It was a few minutes past eight when I saw María looking for me in the darkness. It was so late I could not see her face, but I recognized her from the way she walked.

We sat down. I held her arm and senselessly repeated her name, over and over. All I could say was 'María'; she listened without speaking.

'Why did you go to the *estancia*?' I asked compulsively. 'Why did you leave me here alone? Why did you leave that letter at your house? Why didn't you tell me you were married?'

She did not answer. I squeezed her arm. She moaned.

'You're hurting me, Juan Pablo,' she protested softly.

'Why don't you say something? Why don't you answer me?'

Silence.

'Why? WHY?'

At last, she spoke.

'Why must there be an answer to everything? I don't

want to talk about myself. Please, let's talk about you, about your work, about your interests. I thought constantly about your painting, about what you told me in the Plaza San Martín. I want to know what you're doing, what you're thinking, whether you have been painting.'

Again I squeezed her arm angrily.

'No!' I replied. 'I don't want to talk about me. I want to talk about the two of us. I must know whether you love me. That's all: whether or not you love me.'

Again there was no answer. Maddened by her silence and by the darkness that prevented me from reading her thoughts in her eyes, I struck a match. Quickly, she turned away, hiding her face from me. Then I took her face with my free hand and forced her to look at me: she was quietly weeping.

'Ah . . . then you don't love me,' I said bitterly.

Nevertheless, just as the match was burning out I saw the tenderness in her eyes. Then – again in total darkness – I felt her hand stroking my hair. She said, gently:

'Of course I love you. But why must I say certain things?'

'All right,' I persisted. 'But how do you love me? There are so many ways of loving. You can love a dog, a little child. I mean *love, real love, don't you understand*?'

I had a flash of intuition. Quickly I struck a second match. Just as I had suspected, María was smiling. That is, she was not smiling then, but a tenth of a second earlier she had been smiling. I sometimes have had the sensation that someone was watching me, and, turning suddenly and not finding anyone, sensed that the emptiness around me was very recent, that something fleeting had just disappeared, leaving a slight ripple vibrating on the air. It was something like that.

'You were smiling,' I said in a rage.

'Smiling?' she asked, surprised.

'Yes, smiling. You can't fool me quite as easily as you think. I never miss anything.'

'And what did you notice?' Her voice was hard.

'Something on your face. The trace of a smile.'

'What would I be smiling about?' she asked in the same tone.

'About my naïveté. About my asking whether you really loved me, or loved me like a child. How can I know . . . But you had been smiling. I'm sure of that.'

María stood up.

'What are you doing?' I asked, astonished.

'I'm leaving' was her brusque reply.

I sprang to my feet. 'What, you're leaving?'

'That's what I said. I'm leaving.'

'What do you mean, *leaving*? Why?'

She did not reply. I seized her arms and almost shook her.

'Why . . . are . . . you . . . leaving?'

'Because I'm afraid that you don't understand me, either.'

I was furious.

'Don't understand you? I ask you something that's a matter of life or death to me, and instead of answering, you smile. And then you get angry. What makes you think I don't understand you?'

'You imagined I was smiling,' she commented coldly.

'I'm sure of it.'

'Then you're mistaken. And I'm deeply hurt that you could believe that.'

I did not know what to believe. Strictly speaking, I had not

seen a smile, only something like a trace of one on a face that
was now serious.

'Oh, I don't know, María. Forgive me.' Now I was abjectly
sorry. 'I was so sure you had smiled.'

Dejected, I stood waiting for her to speak. After a moment I
felt her hand on my arm, gentle and tender. Then I heard her
soft and sorrowful voice:

'But how could you think such a thing?'

'I don't know, I don't know.' I was near tears.

She pulled me back onto the bench, and stroked my hair as
she had done earlier.

'I warned you I would only bring you harm.' Her words broke
a brief silence. 'You see now I was right.'

'It was my fault,' I objected.

'It may have been my fault,' she commented pensively, as if
talking to herself.

'It's so strange,' I thought.

'What's strange?' María asked.

I was dumbfounded. Then I believed (and for days afterward)
that María was able to read my mind. Today I wonder whether
I spoke those words aloud, without realizing.

'What's strange?' she repeated, because in my amazement I
had not answered her question.

'It's so strange about your age.'

'My age?'

'Yes, your age. How old are you?'

She laughed.

'How old do you think I am?'

'That's precisely what's strange,' I returned. 'The first time
I saw you I thought you were about twenty-six.'

'And now?'

'I don't know. Even at the beginning I was confused, because something – nothing physical – made me think . . .'

'Made you think what?'

'Made me think you were much older. There are times when I am with you that I feel like a child.'

'How old are you?'

'Thirty-eight.'

'That's really very young.'

I was still confused. Not because I thought I was so old but because in spite of everything I must be much older than she. She could not be more than twenty-six.

'Yes, very young,' she repeated, perhaps sensing my bewilderment.

'Well, how old are you?' I insisted.

'What does my age matter?' she asked, serious now.

'Then why did you ask how old I was?' I was close to irritation.

'This conversation is absurd,' she replied. 'Absolute nonsense. I can't believe you're concerned about such things.'

Was I concerned? About our having this conversation? In fact, how could this be happening? I was so confused I had forgotten the reason for my first question. No, to be more accurate, I had not *analyzed* the reason for my first question. Only when I was home, hours later, did I realize the profound significance of that apparently trivial conversation.

XVII

For more than a month we saw each other almost every day. I do not want to recall in detail everything that happened during that marvelous and terrible period. There were too many unhappy times to want to relive them in memory.

María began to visit my studio. The scene of the matches, with minor variations, had occurred once or twice again, and I was obsessed by the idea that her love for me was, in the best of cases, the love of a mother or sister. I came to believe that only physical union would prove that she truly loved me.

I will say right now that this was another of my many naïve fantasies, the kind of ingenuousness that must often have caused María to smile behind my back. Far from giving me peace of mind, physical love distressed me even more, bringing with it new and tormenting doubts, painful scenes of misunderstandings, cruel experiments with María. I will never forget the hours I spent in the studio. During that whole period my sentiments – given María's contradictions and inexplicable actions – swung between the purest love and the wildest hatred. In spite of the fact that she gave herself to me without reservation, I would suddenly be overcome with the feeling it was all a sham. For a while she would seem as innocent as a young girl, but suddenly

I would be convinced she was a bitch, and then a long parade of doubts would file through my mind: where? how? how many? when?

On those occasions I could not suppress the thought that María was playing the most subtle and cruel games, and that in her hands I was a wide-eyed little boy being lulled with fairy tales to eat his supper or go to sleep. At times I would be possessed with a moral frenzy. I would leap up, get into my clothes, and rush outside for a breath of fresh air, to mull over my doubts and apprehensions. On other days my reaction was aggressive and brutal. I would throw myself on María, seize her arms in an iron grip, twist her backward, and stare into her eyes, trying to force a guarantee that her love was *true* love.

But none of this is exactly what I intended to say. I must confess that I myself do not know what I mean when I say '*true* love.' And the curious thing is that although I used that expression repeatedly in questioning María, I have never until today actually analyzed it carefully. What did I mean? A love that included physical passion? Perhaps I sought physical passion in my desperation to strengthen the bond between us. I was sure there were times we did communicate, but in a way so subtle, so transient, so tenuous, that afterward I was more desperately alone than I had been before, with that undefined dissatisfaction that comes with trying to reconstruct a dream of love. I know that suddenly, sitting in a park at dusk or watching a foreign freighter leaving port, we achieved rare moments of communion. Being together lessened the melancholy that always accompanies such moments – surely the result of the essential incommunicability of beauty. All we had to do was look at each other and we knew that we were thinking, that is, feeling, the same things.

Of course we paid dearly for those moments, since everything that happened afterward seemed gross or dull. Anything we did (talk, drink coffee) was painful, because it pointed out the brevity of those instants of communion. And, what was much worse, they caused further rifts between us, because in my desperation to perpetuate that sharing any way I could, I would force María to make love. All we accomplished was to confirm the impossibility of prolonging or strengthening oneness through a physical act. But María aggravated matters because, perhaps in a desire to rid me of my obsession, she seemed to experience a true and almost unbelievable pleasure. That caused the episodes of my throwing on my clothes and rushing outside, or brutally twisting her arm, hoping to wring confessions from her about the authenticity of her emotions and sensations. And all of this became so abhorrent that when she suspected the moment was approaching for making love, she tried to avoid it. Finally she became totally cynical, and tried to convince me that our lovemaking was not only futile, but harmful.

She succeeded only in heightening my doubts about the nature of her love: I wondered whether she had been acting all the time in order to argue that physical love was damaging our relationship, and thus avoid it in the future: the truth being that she had detested it from the beginning – proving she had been feigning pleasure. Naturally, other quarrels developed and there was no point in trying to convince me of anything; all she did was drive me mad with new and more subtle doubts, and that led to new and ever more convoluted questioning.

What galled me most when I considered any hypothetical

deception was that I had surrendered myself to her wholly, defenseless as a newborn babe.

'If I ever suspect you have deceived me,' I raged, 'I will kill you like a dog.'

I would twist her arm and glare into her eyes to see whether I could detect some sign, some suspicious gleam, some fleeting spark of irony. But she only stared at me like a frightened child, or with a sad face began to dress in silence.

One day when our argument was more heated than usual I shouted a terrible obscenity at her. She froze, then slowly, without a word, went behind the model's screen to put on her clothes, and when, after struggling between hatred and remorse, I ran to ask her to forgive me, I saw that her face was wet with tears. I could not think what to do. I kissed her eyes tenderly; meekly, I begged her forgiveness; I wept; I berated myself for being a cruel, unfair, vindictive monster. And I believed that – as long as she showed a trace of distress; but the minute she stopped crying and a smile started to light her face, I began to find it unnatural that she was no longer upset. It was all right that she should be feeling more cheerful, but it was extremely suspicious that she could feel happy after being called what I called her. It seemed to me that any woman would be humiliated by being called that, even a prostitute. No woman should be able to shift moods so quickly, *unless there was a certain truth to what I had said.*

Scenes like this were repeated almost every day. Sometimes they ended in relative calm, and we would go out to walk through the Plaza Francia like two lovesick teenagers, talking about painting or music; sometimes, in a low voice, she would sing some little song for me. But such moments of tenderness were growing more infrequent and short-lived, like intervals of sunshine in an increasingly dark and stormy sky. My doubts and questionings were engulfing everything, like jungle vines curling around trees in a park, choking the life from them.

XVIII

Every day my interrogations – about María's silences, the look
in her eyes, her hesitant words, her love affairs, a visit to the
estancia – grew more intense and more unmerciful. One day I
asked her why she called herself 'Señorita Iribarne' instead of,
as Allende's wife, 'Señora de Allende.' She smiled, and said:

'What a child you are! What difference can it make?'

'It makes a lot of difference to me,' I said, watching her eyes.

Her smile disappeared, and she said, 'It's a family custom.'

'Ah, but the first time I called your house and asked for
"Señorita Iribarne,"' I countered, 'the maid hesitated before
answering me.'

'You must have imagined it.'

'Maybe. But why didn't she correct me?'

María smiled again, more brightly.

'I just explained,' she said. 'It's our custom, so obviously the
maid knows about it. Everyone calls me María Iribarne.'

'The "María Iribarne" sounds reasonable, but I thought it
was odd the maid didn't seem surprised by the "Señorita."'

'Oh . . . I didn't realize that was what bothered you. Well,
that isn't usual, and that may explain why she hesitated.'

She seemed abstracted, as if considering that for the first time.

'But I'm telling you, she didn't correct me.'

'Who?' she asked, as if she had been far away.

'The maid. She didn't correct me when I said "Señorita."'

'But, Juan Pablo. None of this is of the least importance. I can't imagine what you want to prove.'

'I want to prove that probably it wasn't the first time someone called you "Señorita." The maid would have corrected that the first time.'

María burst out laughing.

'You are absolutely fantastic,' she said almost happily, hugging me tenderly.

I was unmoved.

'Furthermore,' I continued, 'when you first came to the phone your voice was neutral, very businesslike – until you closed the door. Then your tone was affectionate. Why the change?'

'But, Juan Pablo,' she replied, suddenly very serious. 'How could I have spoken with affection in front of the maid?'

'Yes, that part is logical. But you said, "When I close the door they know I am not to be disturbed." That couldn't refer to me because it was the first time I had called. Or to Hunter, since you can see him as often as you like at the *estancia*. It seems obvious to me that there are other people who call you, or used to call you. Is that true?'

María's eyes filled with sadness.

'Instead of looking so sad, you might answer,' I commented irritably.

'But, Juan Pablo, everything you're saying is childish. Of course I talk to other people: cousins, family friends, my mother, how do I know?'

'But I wouldn't think that you would have to hide for that kind of conversation.'

'And where do you get the right to say that I "hide"?' she replied angrily.

'Don't get excited. It was you who told me about a certain Richard, who wasn't a cousin, or a family friend . . . or your mother.'

María was suddenly despondent.

'Poor Richard,' she said softly.

'Why "poor"?'

'You know very well he committed suicide, and in a way I was slightly to blame. He used to write me awful letters, but there was nothing I could do. Poor, poor Richard.'

'I want you to show me some of those letters.'

'Why? He's dead now.'

'I don't care, I want to see them anyway.'

'I burned them all.'

'Then why didn't you say in the beginning you'd burned them? Instead, you said, "Why? He's dead now." That's what you always do. Besides, why burn them – if in fact that's what you really did? One day you admitted to me that you keep all your love letters. Richard's letters must have been very compromising for you to have done that. Am I right?'

'I didn't burn them because they were compromising, I burned them because they were sad. They depressed me.'

'Why did they depress you?'

'I don't know . . . Richard was a depressing person. He was a lot like you.'

'Were you in love with him?'

'Please . . .'

'Please, what . . . ?'

'Don't do this, Juan Pablo. You get the strangest ideas . . .'

'I don't see that they're so irrational. He falls in love with you, he writes you letters so terrible you think it best to burn them, he commits suicide, and you think my ideas are irrational. Why is that?'

'Because in spite of everything, I never loved him.'

'And why not?'

'I don't really know. Maybe he wasn't my type.'

'You just said he was a lot like me.'

'For God's sake. I meant that he was like you in some ways, not that he was *identical*. He was a man incapable of creating anything; he had a lethal intelligence; he was a nihilist. Something like your negative side.'

'All right. But I still don't understand the need to burn the letters.'

'I repeat, I burned them because they depressed me.'

'But you could have kept them without reading them. The fact that you burned them proves you kept reading them until you burned them. And if you kept reading them, you must have had some reason – something about the man attracted you.'

'I didn't say he didn't attract me.'

'You said he wasn't your type.'

'My God, my God! Death isn't my "type," either, and yet it often attracts me. Richard attracted me almost the same way death does, or oblivion. But I don't believe you give in passively to such feelings. That may be why I didn't love him. That *is* why I burned his letters. When he died I decided to destroy anything that would prolong his existence.'

María's mood did not improve, and I could not get another

word from her on the subject of Richard. I must add, however, that it was not the idea of Richard that tormented me, because I came to know quite a bit about him. What tortured me were the men I didn't know, the shadows María never mentioned but I could sense moving silently and darkly in her life. The worst things I imagined about María I imagined happening with those anonymous shadows. One word that escaped from her lips while we were making love used to crucify me – still crucifies me.

But among the many hours I spent interrogating María, one session was particularly revealing about her and her love.

XIX

Naturally, since she had married Allende, it was logical to think that she had once felt something for the man. I should admit that this problem, which we could call 'the Allende problem,' was one of the ones that most obsessed me. There were many enigmas to be explained, but especially two. Had she once loved him? Did she still love him? These questions could not be considered in isolation; they were related to others. If she did not love Allende, whom did she love? Me? Hunter? One of the mysterious telephone callers? Or was it that she loved different people in different ways, as some men do? *It was also possible that she did not love anyone*, and that she told each of us in sequence – poor fools, poor innocent fools – that we were *the only one*, and that the others were mere shadows, people with whom she had a superficial or obvious relationship.

One day I decided to clear up the Allende problem. I began by asking María why she had married him.

'I loved him,' she answered.

'Then you don't love him now?'

'I didn't say I'd stopped loving him,' she replied.

'You said, "I loved him." You didn't say, "I love him."'

73

'You always twist my words, and pervert my meaning,' María protested. 'When I said I had married him because I loved him, I didn't mean I don't love him now.'

'Ah, then you do love him,' I parried swiftly, as if hoping to prove she had lied in answer to earlier questions.

María was subdued, and unresponsive.

'Why don't you answer?'

'Because there doesn't seem to be any point. We've had this same conversation too many times before.'

'No, this is different from the other times. I asked you whether you love Allende now, and you told me yes. But I seem to remember that not too long ago, at the port, you told me I was the first person you ever loved.'

Again María did not answer. What irritated me about her was not only that she contradicted herself but that it was almost impossible to get her to say anything at all.

'What is your answer to that?' I said.

'There are many ways of loving, of caring,' she replied in a weary voice. 'You probably are thinking that I can't still love Allende the way I loved him years ago when we were married.'

'What way is that?'

'What do you mean, "what way"? You know what I mean.'

'I don't know at all.'

'I've told you again and again.'

'You may have told me, but you've never made it clear.'

'Made it clear?' she exclaimed bitterly. 'You have told me a thousand times that many things cannot be explained, and now you tell me I must explain something as complex as this. I have told *you* a thousand times that Allende is my best friend, that

I love him like a brother, that I look after him, that I feel great tenderness for him, that I have the greatest admiration for his serenity, that he seems far superior to me in every way, and that when I compare myself to him I feel contemptible and guilt-ridden. How can you imagine that I don't love him?'

'I didn't say you don't love him. You're the one who said that things aren't the same as they were when you married him. Maybe from that I should deduce that when you married him you loved him the way you say you love me now. But remember that a few days ago in the port you told me I was the first person you ever truly loved.'

María's eyes were sad.

'All right. We'll ignore that contradiction,' I continued. 'But let's go back to Allende. You say you love him like a brother. Now I want you to answer one question: do you sleep with him?'

María's expression grew even sadder. She sat a moment before answering, and then asked in a mournful voice:

'Must I answer that question?'

My voice was hard. 'Yes, you absolutely must.'

'I think it is terrible for you to ask me these questions.'

'It's very simple: you answer yes, or no.'

'The answer isn't that simple: you can have relations . . .'

'All right,' I concluded coldly. 'That means you do.'

'All right! Yes.'

'So you do sleep with him.'

As I said this I was carefully observing her eyes. I had an ulterior motive: this was the moment to settle a number of things. I did not believe she really felt physical passion for Allende (although given María's temperament, that was entirely possible), but I wanted to force her into having to clarify the matter of 'loving him like a brother.' Just as I expected, María was very slow to reply. She was choosing her words with extreme care. Finally, she said:

'I said I sleep with him, not that I love him like a lover.'

'Aha!' I exclaimed triumphantly. 'Then you sleep with him without loving him, but you pretend you do!'

María turned pale. Silently, tears began to roll down her face. Her eyes were dull as ground glass.

'That isn't what I said,' she murmured slowly.

'Because isn't it obvious,' I continued implacably, 'that if you show that you feel nothing, that you feel no passion for him, if you show that making love is a sacrifice you offer in return for his love for you, your admiration for his greatness of spirit, and so on, Allende would never go to bed with you again. In other words: that he keeps coming to you proves that you are able to deceive him, not only about your love, but even your own feelings. You are able to give a perfect imitation of pleasure!'

María was weeping silently, staring at the floor.

When she could speak, she said, 'You are incredibly cruel.'

'Let's put appearances aside; I'm interested in fact. The fact is that you have been able to deceive your husband for years, not only in regard to your love for him, but even your own feelings. The corollary should be obvious even to a beginner: How do I know you haven't been deceiving me as well? Now you can understand why I have questioned you so often about your emotions. I have never forgotten that Desdemona's father warned Othello that a woman who had deceived her father could deceive another man. And nothing has been able to drive that one thought from my mind: you have been deceiving Allende for years.'

And for an instant, I felt compelled to carry my cruelty to its extreme, and I added, knowing that it was vulgar and ugly:

'Deceiving a blind man.'

XX

Before the words were out of my mouth, I was slightly repentant. Behind the person who wanted the perverse satisfaction of saying them, stood a purer and more compassionate person preparing to take charge the minute the cruelty of that sentence had reached its mark – a person who, in a way, even if silently, had taken María's part even before those stupid and pointless words had been voiced (what, in truth, was to be accomplished by saying them?). Even as the words left my lips, that suppressed person was listening with amazement, as if in spite of everything he had not seriously believed the other would say them. And with each word he began to take over my consciousness and my will, and he was almost in time to prevent the sentence from being completed. The instant it was (because in spite of him, the words came out), he was totally in control, demanding that I beg forgiveness, that I humble myself before María and acknowledge my stupidity and cruelty. How many times had that damned split in my consciousness been responsible for the most abominable acts? While one part of me strikes a pose of humaneness, the other part cries fraud, hypocrisy, false generosity. While one incites me to insult a fellow being, the other takes pity on him and accuses me of the very thing I am denouncing. While one urges me to see the beauty of the world, the other points out its sordidness and the absurdity of any feeling of happiness. It was too late, in any case, to heal the wound I had inflicted (this was assured with muffled, receding, smug malevolence by the other 'I,' who by now had been pushed back into his cave of filth); it was irreparably late. Silently, with infinite weariness, María stood up, while her eyes (how well I knew that look) raised the drawbridge that occasionally was lowered between us. I recognized the hard expression, the impenetrable eyes. I was struck by the conviction that the bridge had been raised for the last time, and in sudden desperation, without hesitation, I subjected myself to the most demeaning acts: kissing her feet, for example. I gained nothing but a pitying look, a momentary mellowing about the eyes. But pity, only pity.

Even as she was leaving, assuring me, yet again, that she had no hard feelings toward me, I was sinking into paralyzing inertia. I stood in the middle of my studio, oblivious of everything around me, staring blankly ahead like a cretin, until suddenly I became conscious that I must *do* something.

I ran outside, but María was nowhere to be seen. I rushed to her house by taxi, theorizing that she would not go directly home and that I could wait for her there. For more than an hour I waited in vain. I called her house from a bar. I was informed that she was not in and that she had not been home since four o'clock (the hour she had left to come to my studio). I waited several hours more. I called again. I was told that María would not be home until late that evening.

Frantic, I looked for her everywhere, that is, in the places where we used to meet or walk: La Recoleta, Avenida Centenario,

Plaza Francia, the port. I could not find her anywhere, and finally it dawned on me that logically she would be anywhere other than the places that reminded her of our happiest moments. Again I hurried to her house, but by then it was so late I was sure that María must be home. I phoned once again. She had, in fact, returned, but she was in bed and could not come to the telephone. I left my name anyway.

Something between us had been shattered.

XXI

I returned home with a feeling of absolute loneliness.

Usually that feeling of being alone in the world is accompanied by a condescending sense of superiority. I scorn all humankind; people around me seem vile, sordid, stupid, greedy, gross, niggardly. I do not fear solitude; it is almost Olympian.

That night, like many other nights, I was alone as a consequence of my own failings, my own depravity. At such times the world seems despicable, even though I know that I am necessarily a part of it. Then a frenzy to obliterate everything sweeps over me; I let myself be seduced by the temptation of suicide; I get drunk; I look for prostitutes. I receive a certain satisfaction from proving my own baseness, in confirming that I am no better than the lowest of the low around me.

That night I got drunk in a cheap little bar. At the height of my drunkenness I felt such revulsion for the woman with me, and for the sailors around me, that I fled outside. I walked down Viamonte to the docks. There, I sat down and sobbed. The filthy water below beckoned to me. Why suffer? The seduction of suicide lies in its easy oblivion: in one second the whole absurd universe would crumble as if it were a gigantic facsimile, as if the solidity of its skyscrapers, its battleships, its tanks, its prisons, were nothing more than a mirage, as illusory as the skyscrapers, battleships, tanks, and prisons of a nightmare.

In the light of this reasoning, life becomes a long nightmare, but one from which we can be liberated by death – which thus becomes a kind of awakening. But awakening to what? My indecisiveness about plunging into absolute and eternal nothingness had deterred me whenever I was tempted by suicide. In spite of everything, man clings desperately to existence and, ultimately, prefers to bear life's imperfections, the torment of its sordidness, rather than dispel the mirage through an act of will. It also happens that when we have reached the limits of despair that precede suicide, when we have exhausted the inventory of every evil and reached the point where evil is invincible, then any sign of goodness, however infinitesimal, becomes momentous, and we grasp for it as we would claw for a tree root to keep from hurtling into an abyss.

By the time I decided to go home it was almost morning. I do not remember how but, in spite of that decision (which I recall perfectly), I suddenly found myself before Allende's house. What is curious is that I do not remember the intervening events. I can see myself sitting on the dock, gazing into the filthy water and thinking, 'I must get to bed,' and then I see myself standing before Allende's house, staring up at the fifth floor. What was I doing? It was ludicrous to imagine that I might be able to see María at that hour. I stood there a long time, mesmerized, until an idea came to me. I walked down to the avenue, looked for a bar, and telephoned her. I called without stopping to think what I would say to justify calling at such an hour. When someone answered – the phone had rung for five minutes – I stood paralyzed, unable to open my mouth.

Horrified, I hung up the receiver. I left the café and walked aimlessly, until I was surprised to find myself back at the same café. To avoid attracting attention, I ordered a gin, and, while I drank it, decided it was time to get myself home.

Some time later I was back in my studio. I threw myself, fully clothed, onto the bed and was instantly asleep.

XXII

I woke up trying to scream. I was standing in the middle of the studio. This is what I had dreamed. Several persons, including myself, had an appointment at a man's house. I reached the house, which from the outside looked like any other, and went in. As I entered I immediately sensed that it was not the same, that it was different from any other. The owner said:

'I've been expecting you.'

I suspected I had fallen into a trap, and tried to escape. I made an enormous effort, but it was too late: my body no longer obeyed me. I resigned myself and prepared to observe what was to happen, as if it had no relation to me. The man began to change me into a bird, into a man-size bird. He began with my feet: I saw them gradually turning into something like rooster claws. Then my whole body began to change, from the feet up, like water rising in a pool. My only hope now lay with my friends, who, unaccountably, had not arrived. When finally they did come, something horrible happened: they did not notice my transformation. They behaved normally, proving they thought I looked the same as I always did. Convinced that the magus had cast a spell that caused them to see a normal person, I determined to tell them what he had done to me. I had intended to tell this fantastic experience calmly – in order not to make matters worse with some rash reaction that might anger the magus (causing him to do something even worse) – but when I began to speak it was at the top of my voice. Then I was amazed by two facts: the words I wanted to say came out as squawks, screeches that fell on my ears as desperate and alien, perhaps because there was still something human about them, and, what was infinitely worse, my friends did not hear the squawking, just as they had not seen my enormous bird-body. On the contrary, they seemed to be hearing my normal voice saying normal things, because they showed no surprise. Terrified, I fell silent. The owner of the house was watching me with a sardonic glint in his eyes that was nearly imperceptible – in any case, seen only by me. I understood then that *no one, ever*, would know that I had been changed into a bird. I was lost; the secret would go with me to the tomb.

XXIII

As I said, when I awoke I was standing in the middle of the room, bathed in cold sweat.

I looked at the clock: it was ten A.M. I ran to the telephone. I was told that María had gone to the *estancia*. I was stunned. For what seemed hours I lay on my bed unable to move. Finally I decided to write her a letter.

I do not remember now the exact words of that letter, which was very long, but in essence I asked her to forgive me; I told her I was garbage, that I did not deserve her love, that I was condemned – and justifiably so – to die in utter loneliness.

Agonizing days went by, without a response. I sent her a second letter, and then a third and a fourth, each saying the same thing, but with growing despair. In the last I decided to tell her everything that had happened the last night I saw her. I spared nothing, no detail of depravity. I also confessed how I had been tempted by suicide. I was ashamed to use that as a weapon, but I did. I must confess that as I was describing my debauchery, and my desolation that night standing before her house on Calle Posadas, I felt sorry for myself, and even shed a few compassionate tears. I cherished the hope that María might feel a little of that compassion when she read my letter, and with that hope, I became rather cheerful. By the time I mailed the letter – by certified mail – I was frankly optimistic.

By return mail I received a tender letter from María. It made me feel that we might be able to relive some of the early moments of our love, if not with the original magical luminosity, at least in its essence – using the analogy that a king is always a king, even though disloyal and treacherous vassals have temporarily betrayed and reviled him.

She wanted me to come to the *estancia*. Like a madman, I packed a suitcase and box of paints and ran to Constitución station.

XXIV

Allende is one of those rural train stations with a few men sitting around, a shirt-sleeved stationmaster, a wagon, and a few milk cans.

I was irritated by two things: that María wasn't there, and that a chauffeur was.

I was barely off the train when he approached and asked:

'Are you Señor Castel?'

'No,' I replied serenely. 'I am not Señor Castel.'

Immediately, however, I thought what a bore it would be to wait at the station for the return train; it might be as long as half a day. With ill humor, I reconciled myself to admitting who I was.

'Yes,' I corrected quickly. 'I am Señor Castel.'

The chauffeur could not conceal his amazement.

'Take these,' I said, handing him my suitcase and paints.

We walked toward the car.

'Señora María is not feeling well,' the man explained.

'Not feeling well!' I muttered. My God, but she was good at that kind of subterfuge! Again I considered returning to Buenos Aires, but besides waiting for a train now there was an additional nuisance: the problem of convincing the chauffeur either that I was not, after all, Castel, or possibly convincing him that although I was Castel, I was not mad. Swiftly I reviewed the alternatives, and concluded that whatever I did, the chauffeur was going to be difficult to convince. I decided I would let myself be carried bodily to the *estancia*. Besides, what was to be gained by returning? The answer was simple; it would be a familiar replay of previous occasions: I would continue to seethe with anger, which would be magnified because I could not vent it on María; I would suffer because I was not with her; I would be unable to work – and all to effect some hypothetical humiliation on María. I say 'hypothetical' because I have never known whether that kind of retaliation actually had any effect.

Hunter looked a little like Allende (I think I already said they were cousins). He was tall, dark, a bit thin, with evasive eyes. 'This man is a hypocrite, and totally without will,' I thought to myself. The thought cheered me (or at least for the moment I thought it did).

He greeted me with sardonic courtesy and introduced me to a skinny woman with a ridiculously long cigarette holder. She had a Parisian accent, she was perverse and nearsighted, and her name was Mimí Allende.

But where the devil was María? Was she really not well? I was so preoccupied that I had almost forgotten the two questionable types I had just met. Suddenly remembering where I was, I turned quickly and glared at Hunter, *to dominate him*. This is a method that yields excellent results with individuals of his sort.

Hunter's eyes were mocking, although he immediately tried to hide that expression.

'María is not feeling well, and is lying down,' he said. 'But I expect her to be down soon.'

Mentally I cursed myself for being caught off guard; with

these two I would have to be constantly alert. Besides, I fully intended to take notes of the way their minds worked, their humor, their reactions, their emotions, all of which would be very helpful in regard to María. So, I meant to *listen* and *watch*, and to do that, I wanted to be in the best possible frame of mind. But even though I again congratulated myself on the pair's general air of hypocrisy, my mood remained somber.

'So, you're a painter,' said the myopic woman, squinting at me through half-closed eyes, as if peering through a sandstorm. That grimace, obviously caused by trying to see without putting on her glasses (as if glasses could make her any uglier), merely intensified her insolent and hypocritical expression.

'Yes, madam,' I replied with rage. I was sure she was not married.

'Castel is a magnificent painter,' her companion explained. Then he added a series of flattering, if moronic, comments, repeating the drivel the critics write about me each time I have a show: 'solid,' and all the rest. I cannot deny that as he quoted the clichés I could detect a certain sense of humor. I saw that Mimí was again examining me through her little squinted eyes, and I became quite nervous, wondering what she might say. As yet, I did not know what to expect from her.

'What painters do you prefer?' she asked, like someone administering an exam.

No, now I remember, she asked me that question after we came back down. Soon after he had introduced me to that woman, who was sitting in the garden near a table set for tea, Hunter had led me inside to my room. As we went up the stairs (it was a two-story house), he explained that the house, with some improvements, was virtually as his grandfather had built it on the site of his great-grandfather's estate. 'What difference does that make to me?' I thought to myself. It was obvious that this fellow wanted to give the appearance of being forthright and frank, although for what purpose I could not imagine. As he was telling me something about a sundial, or something that had *sun* in it, I could think of nothing except that María was in one of these upstairs rooms. Perhaps in answer to the inquisitive look on my face, Hunter said:

'There are several bedrooms up here. Actually, the house is quite comfortable, even though it was designed in rather amusing taste.'

I remembered that Hunter was an architect. I wondered what he would consider an unamusing structure.

'This was my grandfather's bedroom; I use it now,' he informed me, pointing to the middle room at the head of the stairs.

Then he opened the next door.

'This is your room.'

He left me alone, saying he would meet me in the garden for tea. The minute he left, my heart began to pound at the thought that María could be in any of these bedrooms, maybe even the one next to mine. I stood like a dolt in the center of the room, not knowing what to do. I had an idea: I went to the wall of the next room (not Hunter's of course) and rapped softly. I waited for a reply, but there was only silence. I went into the corridor and looked to see if anyone was there; I walked rapidly to the door of the next room and, with great trepidation, lifted my hand to knock. I did not have the courage, and practically ran back to my room. A little later I went down to the garden. I was completely disoriented.

XXV

It was when we were at the tea table that the skinny woman had
asked me what painters I preferred. I grumbled a couple of
names: Van Gogh, El Greco. She looked at me with irony and
said, as if to herself:

'*Tiens!*'

Then she added: 'As for myself, I detest larger-than-life types.
I don't mind telling you,' she continued, turning to Hunter, 'that
I am thoroughly bored by great artists like Michelangelo and El
Greco. Greatness is so aggressive, so dramatic! Don't you think
it is almost bad manners? I believe that an artist has an obligation
never to call attention to himself. After all, to claim that one is
original is really like pointing one's finger at the mediocrity of
others – which to me seems in very doubtful taste. I am sure that
if I painted or wrote, my art would never attract attention.'

'I don't doubt that,' Hunter said maliciously. 'Then you would
not want to write, let us say, *The Brothers Karamazov*.'

'*Quelle horreur!*' Mimí exclaimed. She rolled her eyes heaven-
ward, then completed her thought:

'To me, they are the nouveaux riches of the consciousness.
Can you *bear* Russian novels?'

This last question, unexpectedly, was directed to me, but the woman did not wait for an answer; she rushed on, again speaking to Hunter:

'My dear, I have never been able to finish a Russian novel. They are so tiresome. I think there are thousands of characters, and in the end it turns out there are only four or five. Isn't it maddening just when you begin to recognize a man called Alexandre, he's called Sacha, and then Satchka, and later Sachenka, and suddenly something pretentious like Alexandre Alexandrovitch Bunine, and later simply Alexandre Alexandrovitch. The minute you get your bearings, they throw you off the track again. There's no end to it; each character is a whole family in himself. Even you will agree it is exhausting, even for you!'

I felt terribly depressed. People always say that I am impatient. But even today I am amazed that I listened so courteously to Hunter and Mimí's inane comments, and even more amazed that I remember them in such detail. Strangely, as I listened I was trying to cheer myself by thinking, 'These two are frivolous, totally superficial idiots. María could only feel lonely in their presence. *I cannot have a rival in people like this.*' I did not feel any happier, nonetheless. Something deep inside me was telling me to be sad. Worse, being unable to identify the root of that depression was making me irritable and nervous, no matter how much I tried to be calm, or promised myself I would analyze the phenomenon once I was alone. I wondered whether the source of my depression was María's absence, but realized that her not being there was irritating me rather than making me sad. *That was not it.*

Now they were talking about mystery novels: I heard the woman asking Hunter whether he had read the latest novel of the Seventh Circle series.

'Why?' Hunter asked. 'All detective stories are alike. One a year might be condoned. But one a week indicates very little imagination on the part of the reader.'

Mimí was indignant. That is, *she pretended to be indignant.*

'Don't be silly,' she said. 'Mystery stories are the only kind of novel I can bring myself to read. I mean, they are enchanting! Everything is so complicated, and there are those marvelous detectives who know everything from Ming dynasty art, graphology, Einstein's theory, baseball, archaeology, palmistry, and political science to statistics about raising rabbits in India. I adore it when they are so infallible. Don't you agree?' Again she turned to me for my opinion.

I was so taken by surprise that I did not know what to answer.

'Yes, that's true,' I replied, to say something.

Again Hunter's irony was evident.

'I am going to tell Georgie that detective novels – even his series – drive you up the wall,' added Mimí, looking at Hunter with mock severity.

'I didn't say they "drive me up the wall"; I said they all seem alike to me.'

'Whatever you said, I am going to tell Georgie. Thank God not everyone is as pedantic as you. Our Castel here, for example; you like them, don't you?'

'Me?' I asked, horrified.

'Naturally,' Mimí persisted, again not waiting for my answer and again turning to Hunter, 'if everyone were as *savant* as you, life wouldn't be worth living. I feel sure you must have an elaborate theory about the detective novel.'

'As in fact I do,' Hunter smiled, accepting her challenge.

'Didn't I tell you,' Mimí commented sternly, turning to me as if enlisting me as witness. 'Oh, I know this man too well. So, do go on and astound us with your knowledge. I know you are dying to explain your famous theory.'

It was true that Hunter did not need much coaxing.

'My theory,' he began, 'is the following. The mystery novel represents in the twentieth century what the romance of chivalry represented in the time of Cervantes. I will go even further: I think that something similar to *Don Quixote* could be done with a mystery: a satire of a detective novel – just as the Quixote was a satire of the chivalric romance. Imagine an individual who has spent his life reading mystery novels and has reached such a point in his madness that he believes the world functions the way it does in a novel by Nicholas Blake or Ellery Queen. Then imagine that this poor fellow sets off finally to solve crimes, and to act in real life the way a detective in a mystery novel does. I think such a book could be entertaining, tragic, symbolic, satirical . . . beautiful.'

'Then why don't you do it,' Mimí asked mockingly.

'For two reasons: I am not Cervantes . . . and I am very lazy.'

'I think the first reason is sufficient' was Mimí's comment.

Then, worse luck, she turned to me:

'This man,' she said, jabbing her ridiculous cigarette holder in Hunter's direction, 'rails against mystery novels because he is not capable of writing one – even though they are the most boring novels on earth.'

'Give me a cigarette,' Hunter said to his cousin, and only then replied:

'When will you learn not to exaggerate? In the first place, I did not "rail" against mystery novels. I simply said that it should be possible to write a kind of contemporary *Don Quixote*. In the second place, you are mistaken if you think I am totally without talent in that regard. I once had a brilliant idea for a mystery.'

'*Sans blague*,' Mimí limited herself to saying.

'Oh, but I did, I tell you. Now: a man has a mother, a wife, and a little boy. One night the mother is mysteriously murdered. The police investigations lead nowhere. A while later the wife is murdered: same story. Finally, the little boy is murdered. The man is out of his mind with grief, because he loves them all, especially the boy. Desperate, he decides to investigate the crimes himself. Using the usual inductive, deductive, analytical, synthetical, and on and on, methods of those geniuses of the detective novel, he arrives at the conclusion that the murderer must kill a fourth time, on a certain day, at a certain hour, and in a certain place. His conclusion is that the murderer must now murder him. On the appointed day and hour, the man goes to the place where the fourth murder is to be committed, and awaits the murderer. But the murderer doesn't come. The man reviews his deductions: he might have miscalculated the place; no, the place is correct. Perhaps he miscalculated the hour; no, the hour is correct. The conclusion is intolerable: *the murderer is already there*. In other words: *he is the murderer*, he had committed the crimes in some psychic state. The detective and the murderer are the same person.'

'Too original for my taste,' commented Mimí. 'And how does it end? Didn't you say there had to be a fourth murder?'

'But that is obvious,' Hunter drawled. 'The man commits suicide. The doubt remains whether he killed himself out of remorse, or whether the murderer "I" kills the detective "I," as in an ordinary crime. Do you like it?'

'It's amusing enough. But it's one thing to tell it like that, and another to write the novel.'

'That's true,' Hunter admitted tranquilly.

Then the woman began to chatter about some palm reader she had met in Mar del Plata, and some female seer. Hunter made a joking comment, and Mimí replied irately:

'You will have to believe this is a serious matter,' she said, 'when I tell you her husband is a professor of engineering.'

Then they started arguing over telepathy. I was getting desperate because I had not seen María. When next I listened to what they were saying, they were discussing farm labor.

'The trouble is,' Mimí intoned, brandishing the cigarette holder as if it were a baton, 'that no one wants to work anymore.'

Toward the end of this conversation I had a sudden illumination that dispelled my inexplicable sadness: this Mimí had showed up at the last minute, and María had not come downstairs because she could not stand Mimí's and her cousin's opinionated small talk (which surely she must have heard to the point of exhaustion). In retrospect, I realize that my supposition was not a completely irrational intuition but the direct result of something the chauffeur had said while driving me to the *estancia*: something that had gone right over my head at the time, a remark about Señor Hunter's cousin having come from Mar del Plata for tea. Yes, that made everything clear: María, disheartened by the woman's unexpected visit, had shut herself in her room, pretending to be ill. Obviously she could not face someone like Mimí. As I felt my sadness evaporate with this insight, I immediately identified its cause: when I had reached the house and seen that Hunter and Mimí were such frivolous hypocrites, consciously I had rejoiced, because that meant I need not fear any competition from Hunter. Subconsciously, however, I had been saddened to think (that is, *feel*) that María was one of their circle and that somehow she might be like them.

XXVI

As we got up from the tea table to take a walk around the grounds, I saw María coming toward us, which confirmed my hypothesis: she had waited until now to join us in order to avoid the absurd conversation at the table.

Every time we were with other people and I saw her approaching, I thought, 'There is a secret bond between this marvelous woman and myself.' Later, when I analyzed that feeling, I realized she had become indispensable (like someone I had discovered on a desert island), and subsequently – once the fear of absolute solitude had passed – a kind of luxury of which I was inordinately proud. It was in this second phase of my love that all the difficulties had begun to arise. I was like someone dying of hunger, who will unconditionally accept anything he is offered, but later, once the greatest urgency has been satisfied, gradually begins to complain of problems and inconveniences. I have seen émigrés with the humility typical of concentration camp survivors come to this country and happily accept anything that afforded a livelihood, the most demeaning jobs. But is it not rather strange that a man cannot be content with having escaped torture and death? As soon as he begins to enjoy his new security, the pride and vanity and arrogance that seemed to have been permanently obliterated begin to creep back, like beasts driven into hiding – but showing themselves with greater insolence, as if in reaction to the shame of having fallen so low. It is not rare in such circumstances to witness ingratitude and lack of appreciation.

Now that I have the opportunity to analyze my sentiments in tranquil surroundings, I think there was something of this in my relations with María, and I feel that in a way I am paying for the madness of not having been content with that part of María that liberated me (temporarily) from loneliness. That surge of pride, that growing desire to possess her exclusively, should have warned me that I was taking the wrong path – governed by vanity and arrogance.

That afternoon as I watched María walking toward me, pride was almost erased by the guilt and shame arising from the memory of the hideous scene in my studio, of my stupid, cruel, even vulgar, accusation that she had been 'deceiving a blind man.'

I felt my knees grow weak, my face pale and turn icy cold. Why weren't we alone! I would have thrown myself at her feet and asked her to forgive me and to cleanse me of the disgust and contempt I felt for myself!

In contrast, María seemed totally self-possessed; almost immediately my vague sadness began to return.

She was very restrained as she said hello, as if she wanted to prove before her two cousins that we were nothing more than friends. With the uneasiness that accompanies the fear you behaved like a fool, I remembered something that had happened days before. In one of my fits of depression I had told María that one day I hoped to sit on a hillside at dusk and look down on the towers of San Gimignano. She had replied passionately, 'Wouldn't that be wonderful, Juan Pablo!' But when I proposed that we run away that very night, I frightened her; her expression hardened, and she said somberly: 'We have no right to think of ourselves. The world is too complex.' I asked her what she meant by that. She replied even more somberly: 'Happiness is encircled with pain.' I had left her abruptly, without a word of good-bye. More than ever I felt that she would never be wholly mine, and that I must resign myself to fragile moments of communion, as sad and insubstantial as the memory of certain dreams or the joy of certain musical passages.

And now she was walking toward me, controlling every gesture, calculating every word, every facial expression. How could she smile at that woman!

She asked whether I had brought the sketches.

'What sketches!' I exclaimed with fury, knowing my answer was jeopardizing some scheme, a scheme meant to benefit us.

'The sketches you promised to show me,' she persisted, unruffled. 'The sketches of the port.'

I glared at her with hatred, but she met my eyes serenely and, for a fraction of a second, her own softened and seemed to be saying 'Take pity on me.' My darling, darling María! I was devastated by that instant of pleading and humility. With great tenderness I replied:

'Of course I brought them. They're in my room.'

'I'm very eager to see them,' she said in the same cool voice.

'Why don't we go look at them now?' I asked, falling in with her scheme.

I trembled at the thought that Mimí might join us. But María, who knew her better than I, immediately foiled her by adding:

'We'll be right back.'

She grasped my arm purposefully and led me toward the house. I glanced back for a second and thought I intercepted a knowing glance between Mimí and Hunter.

XXVII

I had planned to stay several days at the *estancia*, but spent only one night. The day after my arrival, at daybreak, I fled on foot, carrying my suitcase and paints. This may sound insane, but you will see that it was fully justified.

We left Hunter and Mimí, entered the house, went upstairs to look for the fictitious drawings, and came back downstairs with my paints and a sketch pad intended to represent the drawings. That latter subterfuge was María's idea.

The cousins had left, anyway. From that moment María's mood lightened, and by the time we had walked through the park to the seashore, she was actually ebullient. She was a different woman from the one I had known in the misery of the city: more vibrant, more vital. There was also a sensuality about her I had never seen, a sensual pleasure in colors and fragrances: she would be strangely (strangely to me, for my own sensuality is introspective, almost purely intellectual) excited by the color of a tree trunk, or a dried leaf, or an insect, or the smell of eucalyptus mingled with the scent of the sea. But far from making me happy, this new María depressed and saddened me, because I knew this aspect of the woman I loved was alien to me and must somehow belong to Hunter or some other man.

My depression increased with every step, perhaps partly because of the increasingly audible sound of the waves. When we emerged from the trees and I saw the sky above the shoreline, I knew that sadness is inevitable. It was the sadness I always feel in the presence of beauty or, at least a certain kind of beauty. Do all people feel this way, or is it just another sign of my black disposition?

For a long time we sat on the rocks, not speaking, listening to the furious pounding of the waves below, feeling on our faces the sea spray that from time to time crashed as high as the top of the cliff. The stormy sky reminded me of Tintoretto and his *Saint Mark Rescuing the Saracen*.

'I can't count the times,' said María, 'that I have dreamed of sharing this sea and this sky with you.'

After a pause, she added:

'Sometimes it seems as if we have lived this scene together forever. When I saw the solitary woman in the window of your painting, I sensed that we were alike, you and I, and that you, too, were searching blindly for someone, a kind of companion in silence. From that day I have thought of nothing but you. Many times I dreamed of you here, in this place where I have spent so many hours of my life. Once I even thought of looking for you and confessing how I felt. But I was afraid I might be mistaken, as once before I had been mistaken, and I hoped that somehow it would be you who searched for me. But I helped you with all my heart; I called out to you each night; and I came to be so certain we would meet that when it did happen, when I was waiting for that absurd elevator, I was terrified, and all I could say was something unutterably stupid. And when you turned and left, stung by what you thought was your blunder,

I was half-crazy, and I ran after you. Then came those moments in the Plaza San Martín when you thought you had to explain things to me and I tried to put you off, torn between worry that I might lose you forever and fear of the harm I might do you. I tried to discourage you, to make you think I didn't understand your cryptic words, your coded message.'

I said nothing in reply. Contentment and blackness were circling in my mind as I listened to María's voice, her marvelous voice. I was falling into a kind of spell. The sunset was firing a gigantic smelter behind the western clouds. I knew that this magical moment could *never* be repeated. 'Never more, never more,' I kept thinking, as I felt myself seduced by the vertigo of the cliff and the thought of how easy it would be to drag María with me into the abyss.

I heard bits of sentences: 'My God . . . so many things in this eternity we live together . . . horrible things . . . if we were only this beautiful spot, but, no, we are flesh and blood, sordid and insignificant . . .'

The sea was slowly changing into a dark monster. Soon the darkness was absolute and the sound of the waves below a black magnet. So easy! María had said that we are sordid and insignificant, but even though I knew too well my own immorality, I was crushed by the thought María could be like me – which *undeniably* she was. How? I thought. How many? When? I felt an almost uncontrollable desire to strike her, to claw her flesh with my fingernails, to strangle her with my bare hands and throw her into the sea. I heard other fragments: she was talking about a cousin, some Juan or other; she was remembering her childhood in the country. I thought I heard something about 'stormy and cruel episodes' with that cousin.

I realized suddenly that María must have been making a priceless confession and that like an idiot I had missed it.

'*What* stormy and cruel episodes?' I cried.

Strangely, she seemed not to hear me: María, too, had fallen into a kind of trance; she, too, was alone in herself.

A long time passed, perhaps half an hour.

Then I felt her hand caressing my face, as I had at other times like this. I could not speak. As when I was a boy with my mother, I put my head in María's lap, and for a long time outside of time, a time composed of childhood and death, we were together.

Oh, God! Why did it have to be ruined by suspicion, by things that could never be explained! How I longed to be mistaken, how I wished that María existed only for that moment. But that was impossible. As I listened to the beating of her heart, and as her hand stroked my hair, somber thoughts were stirring in the darkness of my mind, as if awaiting in a dank cellar the moment to erupt, sullenly splashing and grunting through the mire.

XXVIII

Strange events were to follow. When we reached the house we found a highly agitated Hunter (even though he is the kind of person who thinks it bad taste to show one's feelings). He tried to hide it, but it was obvious that something was in the air. Mimí had left, and in the dining room the table was set for dinner. We were obviously late, because the minute we arrived we noticed a flurry of activity by the servants. Very little was said during the meal. I was carefully observing Hunter's every word and gesture, because I thought they might shed light on many of the things happening to me, as well as several theories I wanted to test. I watched María, too. Her face was unfathomable. To ease the tension, she commented that she was reading a novel by Sartre. In evident bad humor, Hunter fumed:

'Novels in this day and age! They can write all they want . . . but what fool would read one!'

No one replied, and Hunter made no effort to mitigate the effect of his words. It was not difficult to conclude that he was irritated with María. But since there had been no sign of irritation before our walk to the shore, I inferred that it stemmed from the conversation we had had there: yes, it would be surprising if he was not annoyed *because* of that conversation – more accurately, because of our long absence. Conclusion: Hunter was jealous, and his jealousy proved there was something more than simple friendship and kinship between María and him. That did not mean that María must necessarily be in love with him. On the contrary, it was more probable that Hunter was irked to see María paying attention to someone else. If Hunter's irritation was caused by jealousy, it would take the form of hostility toward me, because we had no previous relationship. And that is what happened. Even had there been no other indication, one sidelong glance at me when María mentioned the cliff would have been sufficient.

I pleaded fatigue and went to my room almost as soon as we had eaten. My plan was to gather all the evidence I could. I went upstairs, opened the door of my room, turned on the light, slammed the door as if closing it, and then stood in the stairwell to listen. Immediately, I heard Hunter's voice, speaking heatedly, although I could not hear the words. María did not reply. Then Hunter again, a much longer and even more heated comment. María interrupted before he finished speaking, some very brief, low-pitched reply followed by the scraping of chairs. Within seconds I heard footsteps on the stairs. I leapt back inside my room, but continued to listen through the keyhole. In a moment I heard footsteps outside my door: a woman's footsteps. I lay awake for what seemed hours, pondering what had happened and listening for any sound. I heard nothing the entire night.

I could not sleep. I was beset by a series of thoughts that had not occurred to me before. I soon realized that my earlier conclusion had been naïve: I had thought (correctly) that María need not necessarily love Hunter for him to be jealous; I had been lulled by this conclusion. Now I realized that although it was not necessary, *neither was it precluded*.

María could love Hunter, and Hunter still be jealous.

So then: was there reason to believe that something was going on between María and her cousin? Reasons to spare! First, if Hunter's jealousy was an annoyance to her and she did not love him, why come so often to the *estancia*? Ordinarily Hunter was the only person at the *estancia*, and he lived alone (I did not know whether he was a bachelor, a widower, or divorced, although I thought I recalled María's saying that he was separated from his wife; the important thing was that the fellow lived alone at the *estancia*). A second reason for suspecting a relationship was that María always referred to Hunter casually, the way you do when describing some member of the family; but she had never mentioned, never even hinted, that Hunter was in love with her – to say nothing of the fact he might be jealous. Third, María had that very afternoon spoken of her weaknesses. What did she mean by that? In my letter to her I had listed a series of despicable acts (my days of drunkenness and the prostitutes) and she had said she understood, that she, too, was more than departing freighters and parks at twilight. What could that mean except that there were things in her life as dark and despicable as in mine. Might Hunter be one such vulgar passion?

All night long, I mulled over these conclusions, examining them from various angles. My final conclusion, which I considered unarguable, was: *María is Hunter's lover*.

At daybreak I went downstairs, carrying my suitcase and paints. I met one of the servants just opening the windows and doors to begin the cleaning. I asked him to give my regards to Señor Hunter and to tell him I had had to return to Buenos

Aires on urgent business. The servant looked at me with amazement, especially when I told him, in reply to his query, that I would walk to the station.

I had to wait several hours at the tiny station. From moment to moment I expected to see María. I awaited that eventuality with the bitter satisfaction you experience as a child when, unfairly treated, you hide somewhere and wait for a grown-up to come look for you and admit he made a mistake. *But María never came.* When the train arrived and I looked down the road for the last time, hoping up to the last minute that she would appear, there was no sign of her; I was indescribably depressed.

I watched out the train window as the train sped toward Buenos Aires. We passed near a small homestead: a woman standing in the shade of a thatched roof looked up at the train. An opaque thought crossed my mind: 'I am seeing that woman for the first and last time. I will never in my lifetime see her again.' My thoughts floated aimlessly, like a cork down an uncharted river. For a moment they bobbed around the woman beneath the thatch. What did she matter to me? But I could not rid myself of the thought that, for an instant, she was a part of my life that would never be repeated; from my point of view it was as if she were already dead: a brief delay of the train, a call from inside the house, and that woman would never have existed in my life.

Everything seemed fleeting, transitory, futile, nebulous. My brain was not functioning well, but María was a recurring vision, something hazy and melancholy. Only hours later would my mind begin to operate with its normal precision and energy.

XXIX

The days that preceded María's death were the most horrible of my life. I cannot possibly offer a precise account of everything I felt, thought, and did, for although I remember many of the events in incredible detail, there are hours, even entire days, that I recall as cloudy and distorted dreams. I have the impression that I lost days at a time under the influence of alcohol, sprawled across my bed or on a bench in Puerto Nuevo. When I reached the station at Calle Constitución I remember very clearly going into a bar and ordering several whiskeys in quick succession. Then I vaguely remember leaving and hailing a taxi that took me to another bar on Calle 25 de Mayo or maybe Calle Leandro Alem. What follows is noise, music, shouts, a laugh grating on my nerves, broken bottles, glaring lights. Then I remember a terrible headache and being half-awake in a jail cell, a guard opening a door, an officer saying something to me, and then I can see myself walking aimlessly through the streets, furiously scratching. I think I went into a bar again. Hours (or days) later someone took me to my studio. Then there were nightmares in which I was walking on the roof of a cathedral. I also remember waking up in my room in the dark with the horrifying sensation that the walls had expanded to infinity, and no matter how hard I ran, I would never reach them. I do not know how much time went by before I saw the first rays of light through the window. Then I dragged myself into the bathroom and climbed fully dressed into the bathtub. As the cold water began to revive me, I remembered a series of isolated incidents, ravaged and unrelated, like the first objects to emerge from receding floodwaters: María on the cliff; Mimí brandishing her cigarette holder; Allende station; a bar across from the train station called La Confianza, or maybe La Estancia; María asking me about the sketches, and I yelling 'What sketches!'; Hunter frowning grimly at me; I anxiously eavesdropping on the cousins' conversation; a sailor throwing a bottle; María walking toward me with unfathomable eyes; a foul woman kissing me and I, punching her in the face; the itch of flea bites; Hunter lecturing on detective novels; the *estancia* chauffeur. There were also fragments of dreams: again the cathedral, on a black night; the infinite room.

As my head cleared, some of the segments began to flow into others rising from my consciousness, and the landscape began to take shape, although with the melancholy and desolation of landscapes seen after a flood.

I got out of the tub and stripped off my clothes; I put on dry clothing and began a letter to María. First I wrote that I wanted to explain my flight from the *estancia* (I crossed out 'flight' and wrote 'departure'). I added that I greatly appreciated the interest she had taken in me (I crossed out 'in me' and wrote 'in my person'). I understood that she was a generous woman with the purest of sentiments, in spite of which, as she herself had informed me, at times 'baser passions' prevailed. I still found it incomprehensible that a woman like herself was able to say she loved her husband, and me, at the same time she was going to bed with Hunter (I crossed out 'Hunter' and wrote 'Señor Hunter'; I thought the juxtaposition of the words 'going to bed' and the unexpected formal address was very effective). And of course she had the added annoyance, I wrote, of going to bed with her husband and with me. I ended by saying that, as she might realize, such conduct offered serious food for thought, and so on, and so on.

I reread the letter, and it seemed to me that – with the noted changes – it was sufficiently cutting. I sealed it, walked to the main post office, and sent it by certified mail.

XXX

As soon as I left the post office I realized two things: I had not said in the letter how I had deduced that María was Hunter's lover and, second, I had no idea what I had hoped to accomplish by insulting her so unmercifully. A transformation, supposing my conjectures were accurate? That was obviously ridiculous. That a contrite María would come running to me? After what I had done, I surely could not expect to achieve that goal. Besides, I acknowledged that the only thing in the world I really wanted was for María to come back to me. But if that were so, why not say that, why hurt her feelings? Why not tell her that I had left the *estancia* because I was suddenly aware of Hunter's jealousy? After all, my conclusion that she was Hunter's lover – in addition to hurting her feelings – was pure speculation: at the most it was a hypothesis formed to help guide future deliberations.

Once again, then, I had done something stupid, and all because of my habit of dashing off impetuous letters and mailing them immediately. *Important letters should be held for at least one day*, until all the consequences are carefully weighed.

I had one desperate recourse: the receipt! I looked in all my pockets but did not find it. I must have carelessly thrown it away. I ran back to the post office, nevertheless, and stood in the line for certified letters. When my turn came I asked the clerk, making a ghastly and hypocritical effort to smile:

'You remember me, don't you?'

She looked at me with astonishment; she must have thought I was mad. To correct that misapprehension, I told her I was the person who had just mailed a letter to Los Ombúes. This moronic woman's amazement merely seemed to intensify and, perhaps wanting to share it, or to seek advice about something beyond her comprehension, she turned to a male companion, then looked back at me.

'I lost the receipt,' I explained.

No answer.

'I mean, I need the letter and I don't have the receipt,' I added.

The woman and her male cohort regarded each other as two bridge partners might do.

Finally, with the tone of someone completely dumbfounded, she asked:

'You want us to give you back the letter?'

'Exactly.'

'When you don't have a receipt?'

I was forced to admit that in fact I did not have that precious piece of paper. The woman's stupefaction had reached its zenith. She mumbled something incomprehensible and again looked at the other clerk.

'He wants us to return the letter,' she stammered.

He smiled with incalculable stupidity, a smile meant to convey his brilliance. The woman looked at me and said:

'That is absolutely impossible.'

'I have identification,' I replied, pulling out some papers.

'There is nothing we can do. I cannot violate the regulation.'

'A regulation, as I am sure you know, must be logical,' I sputtered. On the woman's cheek there was a mole punctuated with a few long hairs that was truly beginning to offend me.

'And you know the regulation?' she inquired scornfully.

'It is not necessary to know the regulation, Señora,' I replied icily, knowing that the word *Señora* would cut her to the quick.

Now the harpy's eyes glittered with indignation.

'You must understand, Señora, that a regulation cannot be illogical: it was, no doubt, drafted by a normal human being, not by a madman. If I mail a letter and immediately return to ask you to give it back to me because I have forgotten something essential, the logical thing would be for you to honor my request. Or is the postal service hell-bent on delivering unfinished or erroneous letters? It is eminently clear that the postal service is a means of communication, not an enforcement agency: the postal service cannot *force* me to mail a letter if I do not want to.'

'But you did want to' was her reply.

'Yes!' I yelled. 'But I repeat, *I do not want to now!*'

'Don't yell at me; that's very rude. It's too late.'

'It is not too late, because the letter is right there,' I pointed to the sack of outgoing mail.

People were beginning to complain noisily. The old harridan's face was quivering with rage. With true repugnance, I felt all my hatred concentrating on the mole.

'I can prove I am the person who sent the letter,' I repeated, showing her some personal papers.

'Don't shout at me, I'm not deaf,' she protested. 'I can't make a decision of this importance.'

'Then get your chief.'

'I can't. There are too many people waiting,' she said. 'We are very busy here, can't you see?'

'But things like this are part of your job,' I argued.

Some of the people behind me suggested that she return the letter and get on with it. She hesitated a moment, pretending to be busy at some other task. Finally she went into the office and, after a lengthy absence, returned in a bilious mood. She looked through the sack.

'What *estancia* did you say?' she hissed.

'Los Ombúes,' I replied with venomous calm.

After a purposely prolonged search, she held up the letter and began to examine it as if someone had offered to sell it to her and she had serious questions about wanting to buy it.

'All it has are initials and an address,' she said finally.

'So?'

'What documentation do you have to prove that you are the person who sent the letter?'

'I have the draft,' I said, showing it to her.

She took it, looked at it, and gave it back to me.

'And how do we know that it is the draft of *this* letter?'

'It's very simple; let's open the envelope and see.'

She hesitated, looked at the sealed envelope, and said:

'And how can we open this letter if we don't know it's yours? I can't do that.'

People began to complain again. I felt I was on the verge of violence.

'This document is not sufficient,' the harpy concluded.

'Would an ID card be sufficient?' I asked with sarcastic courtesy.

'An ID card?'

She thought that over, again examined the envelope, and pronounced:

'No, not by itself, because all there are here are initials. I will also need proof of domicile. Or, if you don't have that, a draft card will do; your address will be on it.'

She thought better of that, however, and added:

'Although I'd be surprised if you hadn't moved in eighteen years. No, you will need proof of domicile.'

An uncontainable fury finally exploded in me that included María and, oddly enough, Mimí.

'Go ahead and mail it, and you go to hell!' I shouted.

I stalked out of the post office in a white-hot rage. I wondered whether if I went back to the window, I might somehow set fire to the letter sack. But how? Throw a match in it? The match might go out. If I sprinkled gasoline on it first, the outcome would be sure; but that complicated things. At least I could wait for the employees to leave, and insult the old harridan on her way out.

XXXI

After waiting an hour, I decided to leave. In the long run, what would I gain by insulting an imbecile? On the other hand, while I was waiting I had had time to think over a number of things, and was actually feeling quite calm: it was a good letter and it was good that María would receive it. (This has often happened to me: I struggle senselessly against some obstacle that prevents me from doing something I think necessary or worthwhile; I accept defeat angrily and, finally, some time later find out that fate had been right all along.) In fact, when I had begun the letter I had not given it much thought and, at the time, considered some of the insults a bit extreme. But now as I reconsidered everything that had led up to the letter, I recalled a dream I had one night during my bout of drinking: peering from a hiding place I saw myself sitting on a chair in the middle of a dark room bare of any furniture or decoration and, behind me, two persons looking at each other with expressions of diabolical irony: one was María; the other was Hunter.

Remembering this dream, I was inconsolably saddened. I left the post office with a heavy heart.

Some time later I found myself sitting in La Recoleta, on a bench beneath an enormous tree. The places, the trees, the paths of our happiest moments, began to alter my ideas. What, actually, did I have against María that was *concrete*? And as gently as we move a loved one who has been injured in an accident and cannot bear the slightest jolt or movement, the best moments of our love (her face, a tender glance, the touch of her hand on my hair) began subtly to blot out my doubts. Little by little, I sat up straighter; my sadness was turning into anxiety, hatred of María into hatred of myself, and my lethargy into an urgent need to rush home. The closer I came to my studio, the more I realized what it was I wanted: I wanted to talk to María, to telephone her at the *estancia*, right then, without letting another minute go by. Why hadn't I thought of that before?

By the time my call went through I scarcely had strength to speak. A servant answered. I told him I had to speak to Señora María at once. After a brief interval the servant returned to tell me that the Señora would return my call in approximately one hour.

I thought the waiting would never end.

I cannot remember very well the words of that telephone conversation, but I do remember that instead of asking María's forgiveness for the letter (the reason I had called), I ended up saying worse things than those in the letter. Naturally this did not come about illogically; the truth is that I began the conversation with humility and tenderness, but I was soon exasperated by the long-suffering tone of her voice and the fact that she would not, as she never did, answer any of my explicit questions. The dialogue – rather, my monologue – became increasingly violent, and the more violent it became, the more wounded she sounded and the more that incensed me, because I was convinced I was in the right, and that she had no reason to be sad. The conversation ended with my shouting that I would kill myself, that she was a total fraud, and that I had to see her immediately, in Buenos Aires.

She would not answer any of my explicit questions but, finally, reacting to my threat to kill myself, she promised to come to Buenos Aires the next day, although she didn't 'know why.'

'All that will be achieved,' she added in a very faint voice, 'is that once again we will hurt each other cruelly.'

'If you don't come, I will kill myself,' I repeated for the last time. 'Think about that before you decide not to come.'

I slammed down the receiver without another word, and at that moment I truly was determined to kill myself if she did not come to clear matters up. I was strangely satisfied with the decision. 'She'll see,' I thought, as if that would be my revenge.

XXXII

That was an unbearable day.

I left my studio in a fury. Although I knew I would see María the following day, I was depressed and seething with stifled and ambiguous hatred. Now I think it was of myself, because in my heart I knew that my cruel insults were unfounded. But it made me furious that María would not defend herself and, far from placating me, her meek, long-suffering voice inflamed me all the more.

I despised myself. That evening I began to drink heavily, and I started a fight in a bar on Leandro Alem. I picked up the most depraved woman I saw and then challenged a sailor to a fight when he made some obscene joke about her. I do not remember anything after that, except beginning to fight, and then people separating us amid great hilarity. Afterward, I remember being outside with the woman. The cool air felt good. Toward dawn I took her to my studio. As soon as we stepped in the door she began laughing at a painting on one of my easels. (I do not know whether I have said that ever since the scene of the window, my painting had changed: it was as if the people and objects of my former style had undergone a cosmic cataclysm. I will say more about this later, but now I want to tell what happened during those decisive days.) The woman, laughing, looked at the painting and then at me, as if demanding an explanation. As you may imagine, I did not give a damn what opinion the bitch might have had about my art. I told her not to waste time.

We were in bed when I was struck by a dreadful discovery: the Rumanian's expression was identical to one I had once observed on María.

'Whore!' I yelled, pulling away in revulsion. 'God, yes, a whore!'

The Rumanian rose up like a viper and bit my arm hard enough to draw blood. She thought I was referring to her. Overcome with disgust and loathing for the whole human race, I kicked her out of my studio and told her I would kill her like a dog if she did not get out of my sight. She left screaming insults, in spite of the money I threw after her.

For a long time I stood transfixed in the middle of my studio, not knowing what to do, and unable to order either my emotions or my thoughts. Finally I came to a decision. I went into the bathroom, filled the tub with cold water, undressed, and got in. I wanted to be able to think, and would stay in the tub until my mind was clear. Gradually my brain began to function. I needed to think with absolute precision, because I knew intuitively that I had reached a decisive moment. What was the crucial point? Several words came to mind in answer to the question I had asked myself. Those words were: Rumanian, María, prostitute, pleasure, pretense. I reasoned that those words must represent the essential fact, the profound truth, from which I must begin. I made repeated efforts to place them in the proper order, until I had arranged them in this terrible but irrefutable syllogism: María and the prostitute had the same expression; the prostitute was feigning pleasure; María, then, was also feigning pleasure: María was a prostitute.

'Whore! Whore! Whore!' I shouted, leaping from the tub.

My brain was working now with the lucid fervor of my best days: I saw with crystal clarity that I must bring things to an end, and that I must not allow myself to be misled again by María's hurt voice, or her pretense. I must be guided solely by logic, and I must argue through to their ultimate conclusion María's every suspicious word, gesture, and equivocal silence.

It was as if images from a vertiginous nightmare were parading before me beneath the glare of a blinding spotlight. As I threw on my clothes, all my doubts passed before me: the first telephone conversation, with María's surprising flair for deceit and the long practice revealed by her change of voice; the dark shadows around her revealed in enigmatic phrases; her fear that she would hurt me – which could only mean, 'I will harm you with my lies, with my inconsistencies, with my secret actions, with my feigned emotions and sensations,' since she could never hurt me by truly loving me; the distressing scene of the matches; how at the beginning she had avoided even my kisses, and how she had given herself physically only when faced with the extreme of confessing her aversion or, in the best of cases, a motherly or sisterly affection – all of which, of course, prevented me from trusting her raptures of pleasure, her words and expressions of ecstasy; the fact that she would scarcely have acquired her considerable sexual experience with a stoic and philosopher like Allende; her answers that she loved her husband, which only led once again to the inference that she was able to deceive by feigning emotions and sensations; her family circle, formed of a collection of hypocrites and liars; the aplomb and skill shown in deceiving her cousins with the story of the nonexistent sketches of the port; the scene at the dinner table at the *estancia*, the overheard argument, Hunter's jealousy; the phrase that had slipped out when we were sitting on the cliff: 'as once before I had been mistaken'; with whom: when: how?; the 'stormy and cruel episodes' with that other cousin, which also slipped out unconsciously, as proved by her not answering when I had asked '*what* stormy and cruel episodes?' – she had been so immersed in her childhood that she had not heard me, she simply had not heard me, during what may have been her only truthful confession ever; and, finally, that horrible scene with the Rumanian, or Russian, or whatever she was. The filthy bitch who had laughed at my paintings and the fragile creature who had inspired me to paint them, both, at a certain moment in their lives, had worn the same expression. Dear God, how can you have faith in human nature when you think that a sewer and certain moments of Schumann or Brahms are connected by secret, shadowy, subterranean passageways.

XXXIII

Many of the conclusions I drew from that lucid but phantasma-goric review were hypothetical; I could not prove them, although I was certain I was not in error. I realized, however, that until that very moment I had overlooked one important avenue of investigation: the opinion of other people. With grim satisfaction and an intensity I had never known, I hit upon that course – and the appropriate person: Lartigue. He was Hunter's friend, an intimate friend. True, he was as despicable as Hunter. He had written a book of poems about human vanity, then complained because he had not received the National Prize. But scruples were not going to stand in my way. With loathing, but with decision, I telephoned him. I told him I needed urgently to see him; I went to his house; I praised his book of verses and (much to his displeasure, for he wanted to talk about that), I asked him point-blank the question I had prepared:

'How long has María Iribarne been Hunter's lover?'

My mother never asked *whether* we had eaten an apple, because we would have denied it. She asked *how many*, cleverly presenting as fact the question she wanted answered: whether we had eaten the fruit. We, subtly decoyed by the mention of numbers, would say that we had eaten *only* one apple.

Lartigue is vain but he is not stupid: he suspected there was something more to my question, and he tried to evade answering:

'I don't know anything about that.'

And he started talking again about his book and the prize. With true disgust, I shouted:

'What a crime they committed with your book!'

With that I ran from his house. Lartigue is not stupid, but he was unaware that he had said enough.

It was three o'clock. By then María must already have been in Buenos Aires. I called her from a café; I was too impatient to wait till I got home. As soon as she answered, I said:

'I must see you immediately.'

I tried to disguise my hatred, because I was afraid that if she was suspicious, she would not come. We agreed to meet at five in La Recoleta, in the usual place.

'Although I don't know what we will gain,' she said sadly.

'A lot,' I replied. 'A lot.'

'Do you believe that?' she asked in a hopeless voice.

'Of course.'

'Well, I believe we will only hurt each other a little more, destroy a little more the fragile bridge that connects us, hurt each other more cruelly ... I came because you were so insistent, but I should have stayed at the *estancia*. Hunter is ill.'

'Another lie,' I thought to myself.

'Thanks,' I replied dryly. 'Let's plan, then, to meet promptly at five.'

With a sigh, María agreed.

XXXIV

I was in La Recoleta before five, at the bench where we always met. When I saw the trees and paths and benches that had witnessed our love, my mood, already gloomy, became one of absolute despondency. I remembered with melancholy the moments we had spent in the gardens of La Recoleta and the Plaza Francia, and how, in those days that now seemed so far away, we had believed that our love would endure. Everything then had been miraculous, dazzling, but now the world was somber, cold, devoid of meaning. For an instant, the fear of destroying what little remained of our love and finding myself utterly alone made me hesitate. I wondered whether it was possible to cast aside all the doubts tormenting me. What did I care who María was outside our relationship? Looking at those benches and trees, I knew that I could never do without her, even if all I had were those moments of communication, and the mysterious love that united us. The more I thought about it, the more receptive I became to the idea of accepting her love without condition, and the more terrified I became of being left with nothing, absolutely nothing. From that terror was germinating and flowering the kind of humility possessed only by persons who have no choice. I felt an overflowing happiness as I realized that nothing had been lost and that from this moment of lucidity a new life might begin.

Unfortunately, once again María failed me. At five-thirty, alarmed, half-crazed, I telephoned her. They told me that she had unexpectedly returned to the *estancia*. Totally unaware of what I was saying, I shouted at the maid:

'But we had agreed to meet at five!'

'I don't know anything about that, Señor,' she replied, somewhat frightened. 'The Señora left by car a short while ago and said she would be gone at least a week.'

At least a week! The world seemed to crumble; nothing was believable, nothing had a purpose. Like a sleepwalker, I left the bar. I saw absurd things: lampposts, people walking back and forth, as if there were some point to it. How I had pleaded to see her that afternoon! How desperately I needed her! I had been prepared to ask for so little . . . to beg! But – I thought with savage bitterness – when it came to a choice between consoling me in a park and going to bed with Hunter at the *estancia*, there really was no choice. And as soon as that thought occurred to me, I had a suspicion. No, I would say I was certain of something. I ran the few blocks to my studio and from there once again telephoned the Allende house. I asked whether before she left the Señora had received a telephone call from the *estancia*.

'Yes,' the maid replied, after a brief hesitation.

'A call from Señor Hunter, wasn't it?'

Again she hesitated. I took note of the two hesitations.

'Yes,' she replied finally.

My bitterness was now diabolically triumphant. Just as I had thought! I was overwhelmed by a sense of infinite loneliness and, at the same time, insane pride – pride in my infallibility.

I must see Mapelli.

I was almost out the door when I had an idea. I ran to the kitchen, snatched up a large knife, and returned to my studio. How little remained of Juan Pablo Castel's early painting! Now those imbeciles who had compared me to an architect would have something to marvel at. As if a man could ever change. How many of those morons had perceived beneath my 'architecture' and my 'cerebral *je ne sais quoi*' a seething volcano about to erupt? Not one. Now they would have more than enough time to view these toppled columns, these mutilated statues, these smoking ruins, these infernal stairs. There they were, like a museum of petrified dreams, a Museum of Shame and Despair. But there was one thing I wanted to destroy without leaving a trace. I looked at it for the last time; I felt my throat constrict painfully, but I did not hesitate. Through the blur of my tears I saw the shreds of that beach, that remote, anxious woman, that waiting. I trampled the strips of canvas, and ground them beneath my feet until they were nothing but filthy rags. Now that senseless waiting would never be answered. Now more than ever I knew how futile that waiting had been!

I ran to Mapelli's house, but he was not in. I was told that I could probably find him in the Viau bookstore. I went to the bookstore, I found him, I led him aside. I told him I wanted to borrow his car. He seemed very surprised, and asked if something was wrong. I had not thought that far, but told him some story about my father's being very ill and not being able to get a train until the next day. He offered to drive me himself, but I refused, saying I preferred to go alone. Again he showed surprise, but finally gave me the keys.

XXXV

It was six P.M. I calculated that with Mapelli's car the trip would take four hours and that I would be there by ten. 'A good time,' I thought.

As soon as I was on the Mar del Plata highway, I speeded up to eighty miles an hour. I was charged with a rare sensuality that today I attribute to the conviction that at last I would accomplish something definite with María. Yes, María had been like someone behind an impenetrable glass wall, someone I could see but not hear or touch; thus separated by the glass wall, we had lived with anxiety and melancholy.

Feelings of guilt, hatred, and love surfaced and disappeared in that sensuality. I had lied about an illness, and that made me sad; when I called the second time I had confirmed my suspicions about Hunter, and that made me bitter. That María could laugh at frivolous things, that she could give herself to that cynic, that womanizer, that phony, pretentious poet! What contempt I felt for her! I took masochistic pleasure in imagining her latest decision, in all its repugnance. On the one hand there was Castel, and our date to meet that afternoon. For what? To talk of dark and disagreeable things, to face each other once more through the glass wall, only to see our anxious and hopeless faces, to try to make out each other's signs, to try in vain to touch, to feel, to caress through the wall of glass, to dream once more that impossible dream. On the other hand, there was Hunter, and all he had to do was pick up the telephone and call her, and she went running to his bed. How grotesque, how depressing it all was!

I reached the *estancia* at ten-fifteen. I left the car on the main road so they would not hear the motor, and walked from there. The heat was unbearable; in the oppressive calm, the only sound was the murmur of the sea. From time to time the moonlight broke through the black storm clouds, allowing me to make my way without great difficulty up the drive between the rows of eucalyptus trees. When I reached the house, all the lights on the first floor were on; they must still be in the dining room.

The air was heavy with the breathless and menacing heat that precedes a violent summer storm. It would be natural for them to step outside after dinner. I hid in a place in the park where I could see anyone coming down the main stairs, and I waited.

XXXVI

The waiting was interminable. I do not know how much time passed on the clock, that nameless and universal time of clocks that is alien to our emotions, to our destinies, to the inception and ruin of love, to a death vigil. But by my own time it was a vast and complex temporal space filled with figures and turnings back, at times a dark and tumultuous river and at times a strange calm like a motionless, eternal sea where María and I stood facing each other with ecstatic happiness; then again it was a river pulling us back as if in a dream to our childhoods, and I saw her galloping her horse wildly, her hair streaming in the wind, her eyes hallucinated, and I saw myself in my small town in the south, in my sickroom, with my face pressed to the windowglass, watching the snow, my eyes, too, hallucinated. And it was as if the two of us had been living in parallel passageways or tunnels, never knowing that we were moving side by side, like souls in like times, finally to meet at the end of those passageways before a scene I had painted as a kind of key meant for her alone, as a kind of secret sign that I was there ahead of her and that the passageways finally had joined and the hour for our meeting had come.

The hour for our meeting had come! As if the passages had

ever joined; as if we had ever really communicated. What a stupid illusion that had been! No, the passageways were still parallel, as they always had been, only now the wall separating them was like a glass wall, and I could see María, a silent and untouchable figure . . . No, even that wall was not always glass; at times it again became black stone, and then I did not know what was happening on the other side, what had become of her in those unfathomable intervals; what strange events might be taking place. I was even convinced that during those moments her face changed, that her lips curled with scorn and she was perhaps laughing with some other man, and that the whole story of the passageways was my own ridiculous invention, *and that after all there was only one tunnel, dark and solitary: mine, the tunnel in which I had spent my childhood, my youth, my entire life.* And in one of those transparent sections of the stone wall I had seen this girl and had naïvely believed that she was moving in a tunnel parallel to mine, when in fact she belonged to the wide world, the unbounded world of those who did not live in tunnels; and perhaps out of curiosity she had approached one of my strange windows, and had glimpsed the spectacle of my unredeemable solitude, or had been intrigued by the mute message, the key, of my painting. And then, while I kept moving through my passageway, she lived her normal life outside, the exciting life of people who live outside, that curious and absurd life in which there are dances and parties and gaiety, and frivolity. And sometimes it happened that when I passed by one of my windows she was waiting for me, silent and anxious (why waiting for me? why silent and anxious?); but at other times she did not come in time, or she forgot that poor caged being, and then I, my face pressed against the wall of glass, watched her in the distance laughing or dancing without a care in the world or, which was worse, I did not see her at all, and imagined her in obscene places I could not reach. At those times I felt that my destiny was infinitely more lonely than I had ever imagined.

XXXVII

After that endless time of seas and tunnels, María and Hunter were coming down the front steps. When I saw them arm in arm, my heart grew as hard and cold as ice.

They came down the steps slowly, obviously in no hurry. 'Why should they hurry?' I thought bitterly. And yet María knew I needed her, that I had waited for her that afternoon, that I had lived in anguish every minute of that futile waiting. And yet she *knew* that in that very same moment she was enjoying so calmly, I was suffering the tortures of the damned in my personal hell of analyzing and imagining. How could such an implacable, cold, unspeakable beast have crept into the heart of this fragile woman! She could look at the stormy sky as she was at this moment, and walk arm in arm (with that grotesque!), walk slowly, arm in arm, around the park, sensually breathe the perfume of the flowers, sit beside him on the grass, all the while knowing that at that very minute I, I who had waited for her in vain, I who had called her home and learned of her return to the *estancia*, that I would be alone in my black desert, entrails pullulating with voracious worms.

Now she was talking with that monster. What could María have to say to that diseased clown? In what language?

Or was I the clown? Weren't they laughing at me this very minute? Wasn't I the imbecile, the ridiculous fool of the tunnel and the secret messages?

For a long while they strolled around the grounds. The storm was nearly upon us, black, ripped by lightning and thunder. The wind was blowing fiercely off the pampas, and the first drops began to fall. They ran into the house to get out of the rain. My heart began to thud painfully. From my hiding place among the trees, I felt as if at last I was about to witness the revelation of an abominable but often-imagined secret.

I watched for lights on the second floor, which was still completely dark. Soon I saw them come on in the center bedroom, Hunter's room. Everything was normal to this point: Hunter's bedroom was at the head of the stairs and it was logical that his would be the first light to be turned on. Now I should see lights in the other room. The seconds it should take María to walk from the stairway to her room were counted by the violent beating of my heart.

But the light did not go on.

Oh, God! I haven't the strength to describe my infinite loneliness! I felt as if the last ship that could rescue me from my desert island had passed in the distance without heeding my calls for help. My body slowly slumped, as if I had become an old man.

XXXVIII

Standing between trees lashed by the wind, soaked by the rain, I sensed the implacable passage of time. Until, through eyes wet with tears and rain, I saw a light in the other bedroom.

What happened then is like a nightmare. Battling the storm, I climbed up an iron window grille to the second floor. I walked along the terrace to the first door. I went inside and looked down the interior gallery for María's room: a line of light beneath a door led me directly there. Trembling, I gripped the knife and opened the door. 'Why lock it?' I could still think with bitterness. From the threshold, I saw María's hallucinated eyes. I moved toward her, and as I reached her bedside, she said, softly:

'What are you going to do, Juan Pablo?'

Placing my left hand on her hair, I replied:

'I have to kill you, María. You left me alone.'

Sobbing, I drove the knife into her breast. Her jaw tightened and her eyelids closed; when I pulled out the bloody knife, she forced open her eyes and looked at me, humble and sad. A sudden fury gave me new strength, and again and again I plunged the knife into her breast and stomach.

Then I found my way back to the terrace and, as if possessed by the devil, almost fell down the iron grille to the ground. For the last time, the lightning illuminated the landscape that had been ours.

I raced back to Buenos Aires. I arrived at four or five in the morning. I telephoned Allende's house from a bar. I made them wake him, and told him I had to see him without a minute's delay. I drove to Calle Posadas. The Polish servant was waiting at the street door. When I reached the fifth floor I found Allende standing at the elevator, his useless eyes wide with alarm. I grabbed his arm and dragged him inside. The idiot of a servant followed, mouth agape. I had Allende throw him out. As soon as he was out of the room I shouted at the blind man:

'I've just come from the *estancia*. María was Hunter's lover!'

Allende's face was rigid as death.

'Imbecile,' he cried between clenched teeth, his hatred icy.

Exasperated by his incredulity, I shouted again:

'You're the imbecile. María was my lover, too, and there were others!'

I felt a rush of horrible pleasure; the blind man stood there as if turned to stone.

'Yes!' I shouted. 'I deceived you and she deceived us both. But now she can't deceive anyone. You understand? Not anyone! Not *anyone*!'

'You mad fool!' the blind man roared like a wild beast, and rushed toward me, outstretched hands like claws.

I stepped aside and he stumbled over a table and fell. He scrambled to his feet with catlike quickness and chased me around the room, falling into chairs and furniture; he was sobbing, but no tears fell from his eyes, and all the while he was shouting that one word: *fool!*

I ran down the stairs to the street, knocking down the servant, who tried to stop me. I was consumed with hatred, contempt, and compassion.

When I turned myself in at the police station, it was nearly six.

Through the small window of my jail cell I watched the birth of a new day with a cloudless sky. I thought of all the men and women just waking up, who would eat their breakfast and read the newspapers and go to the office, or feed the children or the cat, or talk about the film they had seen the night before.

I felt that a black chasm was yawning inside me.

XXXIX

In these months I have been locked up I have tried many times to think about the blind man's last word, that word *fool*. An infinite weariness, or maybe some obscure instinct, always prevents me. Someday I may be able to do it, and at that time I will also analyze the reasons for Allende's suicide.

At least I can paint, although I suspect the doctors are laughing behind my back, as I suspect they laughed during the trial when I talked about the scene of the window.

There was only one person who understood my paintings. In the meanwhile, these paintings must only be providing more evidence for their diagnoses. And so every day the walls of this hell will close more tightly around me.

PENGUIN MODERN CLASSICS

THE MASK OF DIMITRIOS
ERIC AMBLER

'A gripping thriller … still fresh as new' *Guardian*

With a new Introduction by Mark Mazower

English crime novelist Charles Latimer is travelling in Istanbul when he makes the acquaintance of Turkish police inspector Colonel Haki. It is from him that he first hears of the mysterious Dimitrios – an infamous master criminal, long wanted by the law, whose body has just been fished out of the Bosphorus. Fascinated by the story, Latimer decides to retrace Dimitrios' steps across Europe to gather material for a new book. But, as he gradually discovers more about his subject's shadowy history, fascination tips over into obsession. And, in entering Dimitrios' criminal underworld, Latimer realizes that his own life may be on the line.

'Not Le Carré, not Deighton, not Ludlum have surpassed the intelligence, authenticity or engrossing storytelling that established *The Mask of Dimitrios* as the best of its kind' *The Times*

Penguin Modern Classics

UNCOMMON DANGER
ERIC AMBLER

'A crackerjack spy story, jammed with action, intrigue, thrills and super-villainy'
Saturday Review

With a new Introduction by Thomas Jones

Kenton's career as a journalist depends on his facility with languages, his
knowledge of European politics and his quick judgement. Where his judgement
sometimes fails him, however, is in his personal life. When he travels to
Nuremberg to investigate a story about a top-level meeting of Nazi officials,
he inadvertently finds himself on a train bound for Austria after a bad night of
gambling. Stranded with no money, Kenton jumps at the chance to earn a fee
helping a refugee smuggle securities across the border. Yet he soon discovers that
the documents he holds have far more than cash value – and that they could cost
him his life …

'Ambler combines political sophistication, a gift for creating memorable characters
and a remarkable talent for turning exciting stories into novels of wonderful
entertainment' *Chicago Tribune*

PENGUIN MODERN CLASSICS

FEVER
J.M.G. LE CLÉZIO

In these nine unforgettable and impressionistic 'tales of little madness', the Nobel Prize-winning author Le Clézio explores how the physical sensations we experience every day can be as strong as feelings of love or hate, with their power to bring chaos to our lives. In 'The Day that Beaumont became Acquainted with his Pain', a man with toothache spends the night seeking ways to disown his throbbing jaw; in 'Fever', Roch finds his mind transported by sunstroke; while in 'A Day of Old Age' little Joseph tries to comprehend the physical suffering of a dying old woman. Set in a timeless, spaceless universe, these experimental and haunting works portray the landscape of the human consciousness with dazzling verbal dexterity and power.

'A froth of champagne sentences which display to the full M. Le Clézio's enormous range and vitality' *Times Literary Supplement*

'Dazzling and liberating pages . . . An exceedingly fine new talent' *Observer*

'The author's verbal felicity is amazing . . . we come away awed' *New York Times*

PENGUIN MODERN CLASSICS

THE FLOOD
J.M.G. LE CLÉZIO

François Besson listens to a tape recording of a girl contemplating suicide. Drifting through the days in a provincial city, he thoughtlessly starts a fire in his apartment, attends confession, and examines, with great intentness but without affection, a naked woman he wakes beside. And, as Besson moves through an ugly and threatening rain, his thoughts eventually lead to violence, first turned outward and then directed languidly against himself.

'This terrifying vision of existence is conveyed with intense poetic power'
Guardian

'His distinctive talent is everywhere evident, so that in Peter Green's admirable translation many individual scenes have a horrific hallucinatory power'
Sunday Times

PENGUIN MODERN CLASSICS

AFTER LEAVING MR MACKENZIE
JEAN RHYS

'A break-through book … a novel poised between hope and despair' Lorna Sage

After being left by Mr Mackenzie (and not the other way around), Julia faces facts. Once glamorous and sought-after, she is now down at heel after a string of unsuccessful affairs and leads a jaded, faded life in a tawdry Paris hotel. Then the maintenance cheques stop and she is forced to change her circumstances.

She makes a decision: to return to London to her paralysed mother and worthy, martyred sister. It is to be a new leaf and a new life. But standing on her own is more difficult than she thought – she is restricted by the very existence she has created.

After Leaving Mr Mackenzie is a brilliant, yet brutal, portrait of a woman struggling to retrieve both life and love.

Penguin Modern Classics

A TRANQUIL STAR
PRIMO LEVI

'Works of the highest order of imagination ... remind us why Levi is an indispensable writer' *Sunday Telegraph*

Primo Levi was one of the most astonishing voices to emerge from the twentieth century. This landmark selection of seventeen short stories, translated into English for the first time, opens up a world of wonder, love, cruelty and curious twists of fate, where nothing is as it seems. In 'The Fugitive' an office worker composes the most beautiful poem ever with unforeseen consequences, while 'Magic Paint' sees a group of researchers develop a paint that mysteriously protects them from misfortune. 'Gladiators' and 'The Knall' are chilling explorations of mass violence, and in 'The Tranquil Star' a simple story of stargazing becomes a meditation on language, imagination and infinity.

'We are blessed with this collection' *Herald*

PENGUIN MODERN CLASSICS

FICTIONS
JORGE LUIS BORGES

'One of the most memorable artists of our age' Mario Vargas Llosa

Jorge Luis Borges's *Fictions* introduced an entirely new voice into world literature. It is here we find the astonishing accounts of Funes, the man who can forget *nothing*; the French poet who recreated Don Quixote word for word; the fatal lottery in Babylon; the mysterious planet of Tlön; and the library containing every possible book in the whole universe. Here too are the philosophical detective stories and haunting tales of Irish revolutionaries, gaucho knife fights and dreams within dreams, which proved so influential (and yet impossible to imitate). This collection was eventually to bring Borges international fame; over fifty years later, it remains endlessly intriguing.

'Hurley's efforts at retranslating Borges are not anything but heroic. His versions are clear, elegant, crystalline' Ilan Stavans, *The Times Literary Supplement*

Translated with an Afterword by Andrew Hurley

PENGUIN MODERN CLASSICS

LABYRINTHS
JORGE LUIS BORGES

'Probably the greatest twentieth-century author never to win the Nobel Prize'
Economist

Jorge Luis Borges was a literary spellbinder whose gripping tales of magic, mystery and murder are shot though with deep philosophical paradoxes. This collection brings together many of his stories, including the celebrated 'The Library of Babel', 'The Garden of Forking paths', 'Funes the Memorious' and 'Pierre Menard, Author of the *Quixote*'.

In later life, dogged by increasing blindness, Borges used essays and brief tantalizing parables to explore the enigmas of time, identity and imagination. Playful and disturbing, scholarly and seductive, his is a haunting and utterly distinctive voice.

Edited by Donald A. Yates and James E. Irby

With an Introduction by James E. Irby and a Preface by André Maurois

Contemporary ... Provocative ... Outrageous ...
Prophetic ... Groundbreaking ... Funny ... Disturbing ...
Different ... Moving ... Revolutionary ... Inspiring ...
Subversive ... Life-changing ...

What makes a modern classic?

At Penguin Classics our mission has always been to make the best books ever written available to everyone. And that also means constantly redefining and refreshing exactly what makes a 'classic'. That's where Modern Classics come in. Since 1961 they have been an organic, ever-growing and ever-evolving list of books from the last hundred (or so) years that we believe will continue to be read over and over again.

They could be books that have inspired political dissent, such as *Animal Farm*. Some, like *Lolita* or *A Clockwork Orange*, may have caused shock and outrage. Many have led to great films, from *In Cold Blood* to *One Flew Over the Cuckoo's Nest*. They have broken down barriers – whether social, sexual, or, in the case of *Ulysses*, the boundaries of language itself. And they might – like *Goldfinger* or *Scoop* – just be pure classic escapism. Whatever the reason, Penguin Modern Classics continue to inspire, entertain and enlighten millions of readers everywhere.

'No publisher has had more influence on reading habits than Penguin'
Independent

'Penguins provided a crash course in world literature'
Guardian

The best books ever written

PENGUIN CLASSICS

SINCE 1946

Find out more at www.penguinclassics.com